Frater Dementis

A Novella
By Joe Alaskey

Printed in the United States of America
First Printed, 2016

Copyright © Joe Alaskey

ISBN: 978-0997101812

Deliciously Demented Publishing

Introduction

Joe Alaskey's "Frater Dementis" will cast a horrifying net of insanity over your mind, grip you like a vice with waves of terror, catapult perpetual chills up and down your spine, and leave you searching for the nearest night-light for months and years to come. Joe Alaskey is one of those rare and gifted authors who is not just a writer, but rather a literary artist, in every meaning and sense of the word. "Frater Dementis" is Joe Alaskey's crowning glory and an achievement of epic proportions. The profound and descriptive words that freely flow from the imagination of Joe Alaskey are wildly intense, vivid, fascinating, terrifying, horrifying, enthralling and tantalizing. A showman in life and a brilliant showman on ink and paper, Joe Alaskey proves over and over again that he is indeed one of the most prolific and thought-provoking writers of our time. Joe Alaskey's uncanny ability to transcend unlimited literary genres and styles simply blows the human mind. "Frater Dementis" awaits you...meet him if you dare!

Table of Contents
Beware: Read...Only If You Dare

Chapter One

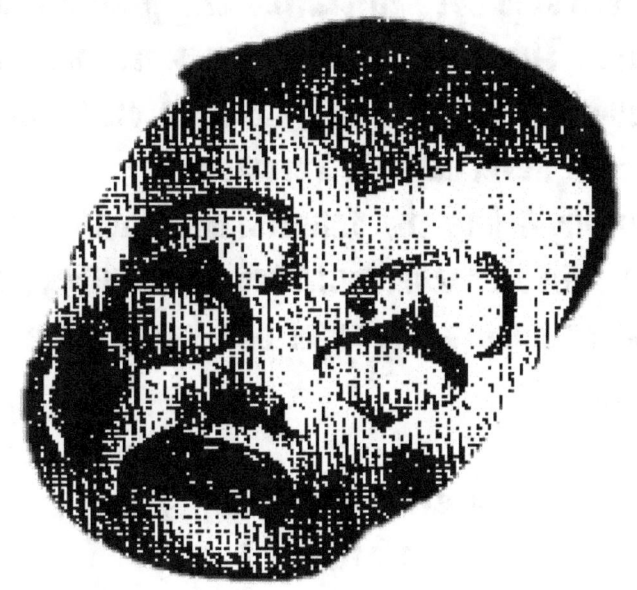

In Congo Square

A thousand and one swirling, looping, mingling colors, gold and red and green and black predominant, and a constellation of faces real and unreal filled Congo Square on a breezy Mid-January noon in 1910. New Orleans' citizens shopped at open stalls for comestibles and patiently patronized a soapbox preacher. Women's merry laughter swam above cheers and children's shouts as a thousand and one pairs of dark legs walked and danced and stood and ran.

This hotbed of activity embraced a sect of voodoo worshippers who, in their own corner, danced the *calinda* with fevered blood, the sexes in separate, writhing lines, to the infectious beat that spawned their celebration. Their agitated intensity escalated as the queen of their sect appeared.

1

She was Crequeline Crozaix, obese, toothless, with fierce eyes. The pattern of the old woman's dress suggested reptilian scales; she pulled the garment tighter around her as she ascended the few steps to a platform that supported her stall, and sat within it.

The voodoo queen sold her self-crafted *gris-gris* to eager steady customers both black and white. These gritty talismans were big and round as oranges and adorned with gaudy feathers. She transacted business with a scowl for one and all, though her eyes never left the ceremony.

Snakes were brought into the dancers' midst and were worshipped.

At length, Crequeline Crozaix muttered something of significance and rose from her seat. She grasped a snake in one hand. Her followers fell silent, awaiting a pronouncement.

And she said it carefully:

"This day... the seed of evil be sown...!
One from the North... shalt bring it forth...
To one of our own, wrongly grown...!"

She sat again, reading and studying signs while returning to her *gris-gris* transactions.

Nicholas, a stern, coal-black Creole in fine livery and pearl-grey hat bought one and, passing through the Square, returned with it to his carriage nearby, a splendid coach with an ornate "D" emblazoned on its door. He placed it inside with his weekly supply of produce and other groceries, mounted the carriage seat and geed his two-horse team.

His course took him down a Storyville street in the chancy Tenderloin District, through *Le Vieux Carré*, and then, on foot, up the steps of the newly-built New Orleans Public Library.

Nicholas entered, venturing past the weather-worn, half-faced statue of Benjamin Franklin, into the Science section. He consulted a list from his pocket, found and collected three books, and checked them out at the desk.

2

In a minute, he was off again. Merging with traffic on a larger avenue, amidst other horse-drawn vehicles, streetcars and a few automobiles, Nicholas joined the flow leaving town, the words of Crequeline Crozaix resounding within him. He wondered what she meant by those strange and ominous utterances.

Nicholas proceeded through the handsome suburban Garden District of Carrollton, where stood palatial estates and small plantations. Lengthening shadows complemented its quietude, he observed, enjoying a warm zephyr against his face. He squinted up at the sunset's purple clouds between indigo sky above and pink below as he halted the team at their destination.

Maison Duquesne was white and pillared and magnificent but for a sense of decay more evident to the heart than to the eye. Even with its colorful, well-tended garden, the knolltop estate seemed somber, remote, forbidding to wayfarers.

As Nicholas brought the team and cargo onto the grounds and the stable behind the house, a shadowy figure at an upstairs window pulled closed the drape...

***

Chapter Two

At the Homerian Society

On February third it arrived.

At a desk in Boston's Homerian Society, William Erasmus Knapp sat before an open copy of his own "Studies of the Inner Mind". He'd been making notes with an idea to expand certain thoughts into theories for a subsequent work. But his mind was elsewhere momentarily, straying into pleasant memories of his meeting with Sigmund Freud only a year earlier, in Worcester.

He recalled Freud's departure when, as they shook hands, the unbound manuscript of his book slid from its container, which Freud deftly caught before it could fan out onto the railroad platform. It had been a memorable visit for many reasons, for all that he had learned, of course, but this was his favorite recollection of the great thinker.

Knapp returned from his brown study to look out the windows; snow fell generously.

His fellow Momerians, some still bundled against the cold without, maintained a genteel buzz of mostly philosophical conversation. A ponder of them stood close enough to the recently-published author for him to overhear their comments.

"Doctor Freud *is* in fashion, isn't he?" twittered Pertwee.

"Merely a fad," grumbled the elder of the group, "Professor Knapp is an opportunist."

"And have *you* read his book, Bythewood?" Frye countered.

The fortyish, earnest-faced Knapp stood, smoothing his coat. Challenging blue eyes peered from under sandy brows.

"No, of course he hasn't, Frye. You can read that in his face," Knapp reasoned aloud.

"I wouldn't give away any trade secrets, Bill," smirked Werlin.

Bythewood produced and began to light a cigar.

"Professor, anytime you want to discuss psychoanalysis, I'm ready," Knapp informed him. "In fact, I welcome your dissent, gentlemen. How else can one progress in Science but through careful examination, trial and error...?"

Bythewood lit a match.

"Careful with that, Professor. You might ignite some old fart."

The conclave enjoyed various levels of laughter.

The young postman arrived. Jonas the age-old attendant took the mail and distributed letters here and there before approaching Knapp.

"One for you, Professor," the dry voice droned.

"Thank you, Jonas."

He scrutinized the envelope. Addressed in practiced calligraphy, it was postmarked "New Orleans".

Puzzled, the professor opened it and begins to read...

5

Her eye on Knapp just outside the door, Celia emerged from Moyers's Millinery Shop with a self-directed smile she shared with the well-dressed professor of science and philosophy, locked the store and took his arm.

"Ah, Celia, there you are."

"Business was fine today, thank you," she teased.

William allowed a quiet, self-conscious laugh.

"What's that letter you're reading?" the attractive young lady inquired.

"Well, it's an invitation."

"Oh, for us? May I see?" Her light brown eyes sparkled with curiosity.

He unfolded the paper in his hand, brushed off falling snowflakes, and read aloud: "It's from a Tristan Beaumarchais Duquesne - of 'Maison Duquesne, Carrollton'. Old New Orleans, no less."

Celia peeked at the letter as they passed beneath an electric streetlamp.

"Old stationery... Bluebloods. With an invitation to what?"

"Ah, well! He wishes to discuss..." he returned to reading aloud: "'very eagerly,' in fact, to discuss a practical experiment in this new-found science called psychoanalysis, of which I have read with avid interest, especially your excellent "Studies of the Inner Mind"'... Bright fellow, isn't he?"

"He must be. I can't past Chapter One," she admitted.

William looked at her with some surprise, at which she smiled back, reclaiming his arm.

"It's not very easy to understand, William," she explained.

"Neither are people," Knapp retorted. "But listen to this -- 'I present, therefore, what may seem as a challenge to you. Should you accept, your modern concepts would be put to the most strenuous test imaginable. I offer myself as a subject for analysis.' Compelling, isn't it?"

"Yes," she thought. "And do you feel compelled to pick up the gauntlet?"

He stopped and considered: "Well, here's my chance to practice what I preach. I admit I'm curious too. Even tempted... What do you think? Would you mind if I go?"

6

"I really – "she began, "I'm sure I don't know...   I'd like to reserve my opinion for the time being, if *you* don't mind, Bill."

"How mysterious...   I wonder what Freud would do."

They both managed smiles as he pocketed the letter.   Then he proclaimed: "I think I'll go."

Celia Moyers felt alarm, her grip on his arm tightening.

"What's wrong with you?" Knapp demanded.   "Why shouldn't I go? After all, I'm on sabbatical.   And now that the book's making money, I can afford to travel on my paid holiday.   You still think of me as a destitute student, don't you...?   Tell me what's disturbing you...   Please."

Face to face, the family-business shopgirl's expression ascended to deep concern.

"Bill, – I had a dream.   You were in a strange city, a very weird place. There were faces, huge faces...   You were surrounded by them, the faces of clowns.   Then they turned into beasts and -- *ate* you, piece by piece!   I know it sounds childish –" she blushed.

He held her close.

"Celia, don't worry.   Your nightmares say more about you than about me, I think...   But...   I also think I should go..."

She looked up at him, unassuaged.

"Frankly, this offer intrigues me.   I almost feel obligated...   Now, while I'm there, I promise I'll keep my eyes open... and stay only a few weeks.   All right?"

"Well, of course, Bill.   I'm sorry I brought it up.   I was just hoping that you might have – time for *me* now."

"You want me to stay," he concluded.

"Not if you *want* to go..."

As she quietly regarded his face, he looked away...

7

In Maison Duquesne, Nicholas silently turned the doorknob to the master bedroom. As he entered he saw the plush maroon bedcurtains and their faded gold brocade undisturbed, the chamber empty. He saw the door within ajar, and entered. He removed the *gris-gris* he'd bought from under his jacket and ceremoniously placed it under the mattress at the foot of the four-poster. He smoothed the lump it made as best he could and exited as noiselessly as he'd come.

The hallway clear, Nicholas proceeded to his next duty. Another door was ajar and from inside, a quiet, troubled young voice stopped him.

"Nicholas...? Was there any mail today?"

Staying outside the open door, his man replied: "Regretfully, no, m'sieur. Surely tomorrow... Are you satisfied with your choice of books this week?"

"Yes, thanks. Though I'm sure I've already read the best books on the subject... Have you been preparing for Anne Adele's visit?"

"Yes, m'sieur."

"I'm glad she decided to come. I hope she'll stay on as she did last year, to keep me company through Mardi Gras."

"Miss Anne Adele will stay on, I'm sure, m'sieur..."

Silence, then – "It's the worst time of year."

"Yes, m'sieur."

A muffled cough ended the conversation.

Nicholas continued down the hallway to the staircase.

***

8

Chapter Three

The Artist's Toast

It had already been a week since Knapp had seen Celia's face by the time his train arrived at the Public Belt Railroad Depot. He thought again about her reticence to see him off, her way of expressing disapproval. But she did go to the station, said goodbye, and even kissed him for good luck. To reinforce their faith in each other. It was good psychology on her part.

Knapp looked at his watch: half the day was over.

Gathering his few pieces of luggage, he debarked and left the depot amid the throng. He boarded a streetcar bound for Chartres and St. Louis Streets, consulted the conductor, and a while later alit in front of Girod House. A doorman and bellboy assisted his entrance, and he checked in uneventfully.

He asked to use the house telephone, and was directed to it, along with basic instructions from the friendly desk clerk.

Jiggling the receiver-hook, he called for the Operator.

"Hello, hello? Yes, the number I want is two-oh-two, two-zero-two, the Carrollton exchange. Thank you."

Knapp resat himself on the hard, narrow seat of this so-called telephone booth off the lobby.

In the downstairs parlor at Maison Duquesne, the bell rang twice. Nicholas answered the call promptly.

"Ahoy. Yes? Who is it?"

"This is William Knapp calling. Are you Nicholas?"

"I am. Welcome to New Orleans, Doctor Knapp. Are you calling from Napoleon House?"

"No, the Girod House. Where I was instructed -- "

"Same place, Doctor... I trust you had a safe and comfortable journey?"

"Good enough, thanks. I've just arrived. And it's not 'Doctor', I'm afraid. Not yet, anyway. It's 'Professor' Knapp."

"Pardon me, Professor..." Nicholas cleared his throat. "Master Tristan is very pleased you've decided to visit. He was most excited and grateful for your letter of reply, which arrived only yesterday."

"Ah. My pleasure. Now, when shall we meet? This evening for dinner, perhaps?"

Nicholas made a tentative sound, then said: "No, m'sieur. With all due apologies, it is not my master's custom to dine with strangers, however welcome they are as guests. He is simply unused to... other people. It upsets him, despite his own best wishes."

Knapp knitted his brow. "Well, I gather that he's -- reclusive."

"Yes, m'sieur... My master suggests that you sample the excellent cuisine at Galatoire's or Antoine's. At his expense, of course."

"Very well..."

"Then," the servant continued, "he wishes to meet with you tonight. Here, of course. After your dinner."

"Oh, I see..."

"I suggested escorting you here myself, but he'd rather not be left alone tonight... He tends to melancholy after dusk."

"I understand." His brow smoothed itself.

"Then you must understand too, that no one is ever allowed to stay overnight at Maison Duquesne... but his stepsister Anne Adele."

"Yes, of course."

"She will be arriving shortly as well, from Baltimore, in case you weren't told."

"No, I didn't know that. Thank you, Nicholas... How would you suggest I get there tonight?"

"It's been arranged, Professor. And it's a pleasant ride by coach. Ask for Mister Mallory at the desk. *Au revoir.*"

Knapp adjusted his legs, shifting his weight with a grimace, and hung up the receiver. Stretching and blinking away his discomfort, he shrugged and exited the curtained booth.

After an hour's rest, Knapp found himself hungry and ventured out onto Bourbon Street. He took his journal with him, strolling and observing the neighborhood until he came upon Bégué's. It appeared to be a charming restaurant and tavern. He looked at his watch and entered.

He took the waiter's recommendation and thoroughly enjoyed his meal. As his place was being cleared, he sipped his native drink and watched some of the locals at their large, central table. They were a clique of "Bohemians" to Knapp, artistic types whose style of dress and behavior were colorful, uninhibited, and unmistakable.

He caught some of their names from their boisterous conversation. The Gypsy girl was Madeleine, Karl the stocky, rough-hewn Aryan, and that lanky, mercurial fellow in the brightly-stained smock with one leg up on a chair was Gilbert Thorndike, the ringleader apparent. Their round of toasts prompted the Professor to order a second Sazerac cocktail.

"I drink a solemn toast to our late friend and literary genius, O. Henry!" trumpeted the fat one in the beret.

"To O. Henry!" echoed Thorndike.

They guzzled; Knapp sipped.

Karl staggered to his feet. "I drink to Tom Edison, who's lighted our way into the Twentieth Century!"

"And shows us the way home at night!" Madeliene added, followed by a hiccup and ensuing laughter. "It's an Age of Miracles!" she concluded.

Gilbert Thorndike sat up. "Miracles...? I object! And at the same time, I agree... I agree because this benighted city is just now awakening from the Dark Age of Ignorance and *needs* some miracles...! And I *object* because...when I am with the beauteous Madeleine, I *like* it dark!" Stroking his long mustache, he lurched forward for a kiss which nearly knocked them both to the floor.

"What we really need are fewer aristocrats!" decided Karl, independent of context.

Professor Knapp regarded them with interest, his chin resting in a curled palm.

"And more artists!" shouted another female.

"Hear, hear!" gurgled the fat man.

"I know what *I* need!" leered Thorndike at Madeleine's breast, which cued more sniggering and guffaws.

A momentary respite in the frivolities emboldened Knapp to speak on impulse: "I beg your pardon?" he interrupted gently. "Excuse me, but --"

"Oh, did we offend Your Majesty?" sneered Madeleine while Thorndike fondled her openly.

"Tourist," mumbled Karl.

"Not at all. But on the subject of aristocrats, do you know the Duquesne family of Carrollton?"

Thorndike belched suddenly, loudly, amusing his cronies no end. Then he grunted a single, derisive laugh.

"No one's familiar with the Duquesnes," Karl said.

"Are you one of their noble line, m'sieur?" asked a now-curious Madeleine, reseating herself primly.

"No. I have — business with them."

"You mean "him", don't you?" blurted Thorndike. "The old man's dead. Only his son, that miserable soul, survives."

"Well, there was a girl too," volunteered someone.

""That's right!" boomed the artist holding sway. "Whatever became of her? I knew the father. Étienne Duquesne, the printer. Once brought him some sketches. "Not good enough! Too blotchy!' says he. 'Smeared!' The old bastard! He knew nothing about Art!"

"Still, you had to feel sorry for them," Madeleine recalled. "The girl ran away from home. And that poor son -- "

"Tristan?" Knapp asked.

"Yes, a sad case," Madeleine went on. "The victim of a contagious disease, they say."

"I heard the family doctor died of it," the obese toper in the beret contributed.

"You'd better be careful, Mister --?" Thorndike prompted.

"My name is Knapp."

"And I am Thorndike, the artist, sculptor, lover of beauty and mystery... Mister Knapp, this boy's disease, they say, is so advanced that he can't even show his face in public! Hasn't left his house in twenty-odd years! And let me tell you something else...!" He leaned forward for emphasis. "I have heard... that he has *no face left at all!*"

"Stop trying to frighten the man!" chided Madeleine. To Knapp, she said: "That can't be so. But I have heard that he wears a *hood!*"

Everyone present felt significance in that.

"A hood?! Is that true?!" blared Thorndike.

"I heard it from one of the witch-queen's boys!" Madeleine held all spellbound. "She sells the butler charms, one every week! The boy works for the tailor too, and told me that once the butler brought the hood in to be re-stitched. It was torn like by a wildcat! The boy had to make another."

Professor Knapp stood.

"Where are you going, sir?" Thorndike wondered.

Knapp smiled wryly: "To meet the monster... Thank you for your information."

"It's not 'information', Mister Knapp. 'S'just gossip." Thorndike rambled. "We have so few amusements, we artists. All you heard from us tonight... is rumor. But you'll soon see for yourself, eh? Come back to Bégué's tomorrow night and tell us all about him! Will you do that, sir?"

Another impulse informed the psychoanalyst he did not like this Thorndike fellow.

"I'm not sure that I will, no."

Gibert Thorndike eyed Knapp differently. "As you say, sir... in any event, I wish you – We all wish you – a most enchanting evening with the Living Medusa!"

More spirited laughter, some nervous, arose.

"Thank you." With a wan smile, Knapp bid them "Good night," and left.

Thorndike stood and bowed with forced irony, and announced: "My friends, an inspiration! I, Thorndike, will render our monster in stone! – Or on canvas. I don't know which yet, but either way, I tell you: I will go to the dreaded Maison Duquesne... and meet the Medusa face-to-face!" He bent low to kiss his girl's cheek. *"Vis-a-vis!* I drink to it!"

Madeleine rolled her eyes and blessed herself. "Oh, Lord God!" she moaned.

"Unless you talk me out of it!"

He pulled her under the table, a tankard in his other hand. Lascivious laughter filled the tavern.

***

Chapter Four

Arrival At Maison Duquesne

Riding in the open Carrollton coach en route to the Garden District, Knapp jotted down an entry in his journal and read it back to himself in a whisper: "'The Gypsy girl says he wears a hood.' A *hood!*"

Ruddy-faced Mr. Mallory maintained a comfortable pace while his passenger took in the lush, moonlit scenery, splendid even at night.

Presently, the carriage came to a halt before Maison Duquesne. Knapp inspected the facade with a forgiving eye as he paid the coachman, who let his carriage depart rather more rapidly than it had approached.

The Professor advanced toward the front door, and it opened, Nicholas silhouetted in its frame by the sparse light from within. He took a tighter grip of his journal. They met on the long, weathered porch face-to-face. Knapp extended his hand but the servant stood still.

16

"Welcome to Maison Duquesne, m'sieur."

"Thank you, Nicholas. I recognize your voice."

"Yes, m'sieur. Please come in."

They went inside, Nicholas closing the door.

Knapp nodded approval of the tasteful foyer as Nicholas took his hat and coat.

"Napoleon House is to your liking, I trust?"

"This one too. It's a magnificent home, isn't it?"

"Yes, m'sieur. Follow me, please. I'll show you about."

They traversed several outer rooms' dark, rich interiors, coming finally to the downstairs parlor where sat Anne Adele Duquesne, tall and graceful, awaiting their entrance.

Knapp saw her unadorned aspect as prim, her outlook of weary despair, but beautiful, with her auburn hair and blue eyes. He judged her to be his age, at least.

"Ma'm'selle, Professor William Knapp. Professor, Miss Anne Adele Duquesne."

"Pleased to meet you, Miss Duquesne."

"Professor," she rose and curtseyed.

"I'll tell Master Tristan you're here."

With Nicholas' exit, an awkward moment passed between male and female parties.

"I must admit I'm rather confused, Professor. Your being here, I mean. I hadn't been told -- "

"Perhaps I should explain -- "

She re-routed his direction.

"Nicholas told me who you are, Professor... And why you are here. And I'm thrilled at the notion of helping Tristan. Yet, at the same time, I'm frightened for him."

"Miss Duquesne, I'm here to help your brother -- "

17

"Tristan is my *step*brother, Professor."

"Oh, yes. – I'm here to help because he *asked* for my help. D'you understand?"

She pointed to his armful of writings.

"Is that your book? "Studies of the Mind?""

"" – of the Inner Mind". No, this is my journal. I carry it everywhere, I'm afraid. I'll be taking notes daily on his progress."

Anne Adele heaved a sigh, then offered: "All his life, books have been his only real comfort. But now he wants to see the world he's only read about... I hope the strain of this meeting won't weigh too heavily on either of you."

"I shall strive to avoid that, trust to it."

"And so, with your kind permission, I will stay tonight and through the morning to help ease that strain," she suggested.

"Fine."

Nicholas returned. "Master Tristan requests that you join him in the upstairs parlor."

"He feels more secure there," said Anne Adele.

"Yes, of course," conceded Knapp.

Led by Nicholas, they ascended the curving staircase.

"I hope his ways won't frighten or dissuade you," the stepsister remarked to Knapp. "He's really quite dear..."

At the top of the stairs, Nicholas opened the upstairs parlor door and entered. Anne Adele followed him in, while Knapp hovered at the threshold for the moment, seeing first how much darker this parlor was. He noticed that it was more sparsely furnished, and that a door within was ajar.

A large armchair at the far end of the room, its back turned away from an unlit fireplace, and several smaller chairs surrounded the table at the center.

As in the downstairs parlor, the curtains before a bay window in the far wall were also drawn closed.

Further, nothing had been placed against the walls, not even pictures.

Anne Adele seated herself at the table as Nicholas lightly tapped on the partially open door.

Professor Knapp took a seat beside Miss Duquesne as they all awaited a response.

Presently, the door inched open slowly, revealing only shadows, and the foot of the four-poster within.

Nicholas stepped aside and took his stand by the hallway door.

Knapp couldn't help but peer curiously into the shadows.

After a moment, Tristan Beaumarchais Duquesne, of average size but imposing by his dint of innate silence and stillness, entered and stood before them, uncertainly, just inside the doorway. And he did indeed wear a hood, one of black silk.

Knapp observed that the face inside the hood was quite handsome, save for the darkness circling his large, grey eyes and the miserable expression that marked his brow.

The stranger merely stood --

-- and Tristan immediately backed up against the wall with a short gasp and a thump! Breathing heavily, he shook off his sudden fear and proceeded to sidle, crablike, alongside that wall and the next, gliding to a stop near the window curtain's edge.

Anne Adele arose as well, and Knapp spoke: "I'm sorry. I didn't realize --"

Nicholas broke in: "Professor William E. Knapp, m'sieur."

The eccentric youth was articulate: "Quite all right, Professor. It may take me a few moments to -- accustom myself to your presence."

The strange young man held out a hand tentatively towards Anne Adele, who neared him slowly. At arms' length, they joined hands.

"Thank you, Anne Adele," Tristan murmured.

19

"Tristan," she dared, "would you like to shake hands with Professor Knapp?"

Tristan swallowed. "I – Yes, I would."

"Come, Professor."

Knapp stepped cautiously around the furniture toward Tristan and, with slow measure, offered his hand in greeting.

Anne Adele stepped back and stood alongside Nicholas.

Tristan shivered a little, then abruptly grasped Knapp's hand in both of his.

"I'm truly delighted to welcome you, sir! Thank you for accepting my invitation!"

He let go of his hand just as suddenly.

Knapp fought his internal discomfort with a quick reply: "I can't resist a challenge, really... You obviously understood what you read. And personally, it was the most compelling letter I'd ever received, so... thanks."

Anne Adele smiled at her stepbrother with approval, catching his eye.

The hooded countenance of Tristan flashed a tight smile back at her; he strove bravely to continue the conversation.

"Your book was enlightening! Encouraging... I should also congratulate you for your courage in coming here under these unusual circumstances. I admire you, Professor, and I hope to demonstrate my gratitude by co-operating with you to the best of my ability. – Nicholas?"

"Yes, m'sieur?"

"Something to drink for us, I think," the young master directed. "What shall we have? Some tea? Wine, perhaps?"

Anne Adele said: "Tea sounds restful, thank you."

"Professor?"

"That'll be fine, thank you, Nicholas." Knapp turned to Tristan. "And you don't have to call me 'Professor'. I might confuse you with one of my students and make you clap erasers."

20

Tristan, perplexed by this comment, smiled shyly and lowered his eyes as Nicholas departed.

Knapp continued: "I wonder how a self-described recluse manages to be such a good host."

Tristan blushed: "It's the way I've always imagined greeting... a friend."

"I hope we *can* be friends, Tristan."

Their troubled host went to the window, then closely along the walls to his armchair a specific distance from his guests.

"That's why I asked you here, Professor Knapp. When I read your book, -- a couple of weeks ago it was, -- I knew I had to meet you... " He sat. "It seemed it was written just for me. It seemed only you could help me."

He looked sadly up at his visitor.

"I thank you for your kind words, Tristan..." Knapp measured his words, "But do you realize that you have already helped yourself...? In conquering your fears by inviting me here to your home?"

"Yes... I had to. So you could learn all about my affliction, but... I -- "

"There are remedies for many ills..." Knapp began, then changed tactics: "What *is* this mysterious affliction of yours, that it should keep you indoors all your life? -- As you've claimed?"

Tristan was speechless, hemming and hawing, sputtering as if he'd suddenly broken down like a motorcar's engine. He blushed redder than before. Anne Adele stirred as Knapp pressed on: "Why *do* you wear that hood?"

The young man stood, stammering: "I'm afraid I... can't say. I won't. I can't. It's too soon."

"Why? I thought you wanted my help."

"I really don't see how this -- " Anne Adele tried to say.

"But I *will!*" Tristan shouted. "When I think you know me well enough! When we know each other better, -- "

"Why wait? Tell me now," Knapp finished coldly.

Tristan seemed dumbstruck anew, paralyzed with bewilderment and fear.

Anne Adele defended: "Professor Knapp, *please!* Not even Nicholas knows that...! And thanks to our late parents, *neither do I..."*

Knapp turned to her. "You have no idea?" -- and to Tristan: "Is this true?"

"Yes!" Tristan admitted. "Since Doctor Perrault died, -- "

" -- only Tristan knows why he wears that hood," his stepsister finished for him. "And I won't allow such bullying tactics -- !"

Now Tristan interrupted, standing between them. "Anne Adele, no... Please. It's all right. This is how the treatment works...!" He sat again, exhilarated, and spread his palms open. "Everyone be seated again, please."

William Knapp and Anne Adele Duquesne regarded each other and sat. Nicholas entered with the tea and served.

"Thank you, Nicholas. Please stay."

"Yes, m'sieur." Again, he stood by the hallway door.

"Professor Knapp, I wish to make a formal offer for your services," said Tristan.

"I'm happy to see I didn't intimidate you," Knapp confessed to him. For Anne Adele, he added: "It was necessary, you see."

A flock of daws flew noisily by outdoors.

Tristan re-adjusted his clothing, and lastly his hood, before proclaiming: "I want you to take me on as a patient, Knapp. For however long it takes. Tell me what I need to do... And when your psychoanalysis has begun to correct my... faults, and I've taken steps to leave this house, then... I'll share my terrible secret with you, -- I promise."

The Professor stood by his side.

"As long as you comprehend, Tristan, that this secret, whatever it is, must be shared eventually -- with anyone and everyone -- if you are ever to leave these walls... And sharing it must be something that *you* want... You understand?"

Tristan nodded in agreement.

22

"For now, I don't need to know the actual nature of this... affliction," Knapp realized. "We have time."

"Thank you, Knapp," Tristan wept. "I'm sorry... It will take time, I'm afraid."

Knapp regretted seeing his tears, and felt obliged to say: "In other words, I accept your offer."

"Ah, thank you, Knapp! I hoped you would!"

Knapp paced a bit. "Here are my terms: I'll visit you daily until some noticeable progress is made, and if none is forthcoming, in my opinion, I'm free to resign anytime and return to Boston."

"Paid in full for your trouble."

"You're every generous."

"It's the least I could do."

Anne Adele rejoined the negotiations. "And it makes sense, we've decided, that you stay at the Carrollton Hotel; it's nearby."

Knapp offered his hand again to Tristan with: "Let's shake on it."

The young man stood once more, and once more, hesitating only a second or two before lunging forward, grabbing and vigorously shaking Knapp's hand with both of his. Then he let go and retreated to the wall.

"You must be brave, Tristan," Knapp instructed. "Only through self-understanding can your problems be solved."

"And faith in God," Anne Adele assured them.

Knapp looked at her as Tristan nodded in assent.

"But now you look tired, young man," Professor Knapp intoned. "I advise you to rest, and... we can begin tomorrow, hm?"

"Yes... I'm exhausted," Tristan allowed. "I'll see you tomorrow... Anne, I'll see you at supper. Excuse me..."

The hooded one took his leave, gliding alongside the walls and into his bedroom, shutting the door behind him.

At the parlor doors, Knapp, Anne Adele and Nicholas converged.

23

"When you are ready to leave, m'sieur, I'll bring the carriage 'round."

"Thank you, Nicholas."

The butler preceded the others descending the staircase.

Knapp asked Anne Adele: "Are you and your brother religious?"

"I go to services but Tristan, understandably, does not. Like our father, he believes that God has abandoned him... Yet he's kept some shred of faith, I hope. I find faith in God very comforting -- in so wicked a world."

"It could only help..." the psychoanalyst said. "Can you tell me a little about his medical background?"

"Nicholas can give you the address of Doctor -- the late Doctor Perrault. I'm sure that'll help," she smiled.

"Yes, it should. Thank you. Good night."

"Good night, Professor."

He waited for Nicholas to drive the Duquesne coach to him. As he stepped up into it and took his seat beside Nicholas, an upstairs curtain slid aside. Anne Adele watched the carriage depart, into the starry night sky, the moon above a sharp crescent.

Nicholas drove the team at a steady clip. Knapp, the open journal in his lap, pencil in hand, heard and wrote down the servant's answer to his last question.

"The other bedrooms were put downstairs by M'sieur Étienne years ago, to ensure Master Tristan's privacy, of course."

"I see. By the way, I'll need Doctor Perrault's address."

"Why?" The question surprised him.

"'Why'-? In order to examine my patient's medical file."

"You will be wasting your time."

"Really...! And why is that?"

Nicholas tightened his grip on the reins. "M'sieur, I love Master Tristan. I have my own method of helping."

Knapp pondered this taciturn answer a moment.

"You are a good man," Nicholas averred. "I have decided... I will help you whichever way I can.'

"I appreciate that, Nicholas. Thank you."

"M'sieur Étienne made me burn the medical file years ago, just after Master Tristan was born."

"I see," Knapp frowned. "Thanks again."

"You're welcome, m'sieur," Nicholas stated without a jot of irony, though he smiled privately, Knapp noticed.

Professor Knapp rode silently, thinking.

He was still deep in thought as later, in his Girod House rooms, he wrote in his journal by gaslight until a yawn guided him to close the book, rise and retire.

Getting into bed, he mimicked Nicholas' plummy voice to himself: "I have my own method of helping!"

Now he is standing on a windy Mediterranean shore, journal in hand, regarding a huge, burgeoning bank of clouds high above a rocky islet across the water, rolling his way.

The sun blinds him; he shields his eyes, looks down, and is surprised to see that he is dressed in his heavy greatcoat, the one he wore when seeing off Freud at the Worcester Depot.

Looking up, he finds that he is suddenly on the islet, facing a deep cave nestled in a hill of jagged boulders. Startled, he loses his grip on the journal, loose pages spilling out in a perfect fan at his feet. He bends to retrieve them, but a perverse gust descends and scatters the paper.

A sound - the faint hissing and rattling of snakes from within the cave - forces his spine upright in terror. He recoils, bracing himself against one side of the stony entrance.

And now he is some distance inside the cave. Shocked, he turns; the sun is a mere patch in the hole behind him.

He hears the snakes again, nearer now.

He discerns a black shape moving toward him.

He bolts for the entrance, but the dark figure darts sideways into his path, now face-to-face with him!

It is Tristan, revealed as the Medusa, its serpents writhing beneath its hood, its face a gloating mask of evil triumphant!

He steps back, breathless with horror. The Medusa hisses a laugh and reaches slowly up to its hood. He averts his gaze, only to see --

-- Gilbert Thorndike, grinning, almost totally turned to stone. Yet he manages to speak: "The... Living... Medusa!" -- and laughs, though his throat contracts with a death-rattle before ossifying completely!

He turns away, eyes shut tight, mouth agape. He tries to run but can't even move!

Again, the Gorgon laughs.

He dares to look down at his own feet and sees his legs turning to stone! He looks up with a gasp --

The Medusa advances, its snakes revealed, now ready to strike!

He shuts his eyes and screams!

Knapp bolted awake, heaving, a cold sweat upon his brow. He calmed himself by degrees and wiped his forehead with the corner of his bedsheet.

***

Chapter Five

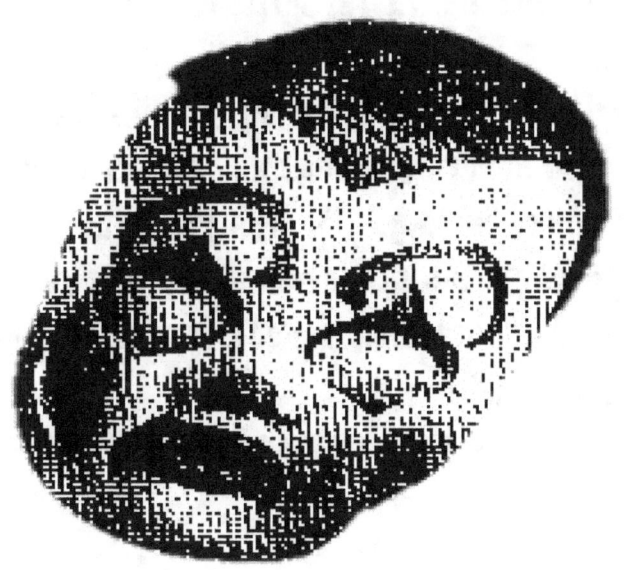

The Nature of Tristan's Secret

Later that morning, Professor Knapp sat in the downstairs parlor, already at work on his journal, sunlight streaming in over his shoulder.

Nicholas and Tristan entered, the latter as nervous as before. From the former, a perfunctory: "Master Tristan."

The young Duquesne moved along the wall, came to a chair and sat. Knapp observed him gesture toward the window for Nicholas to close the drape, which was done.

"Welcome again, Knapp."

"Thank you again. I see Miss Anne is absent today."

"At my request."

"Good. These sessions should be private anyway," Knapp said. "Our first official session, certainly."

27

Tristan turned: "That'll be all for now, Nicholas. I'll call you if I need you."

With a curt nod, the servant left the two alone.

Knapp inspected Tristan's present demeanor, and reset his journal in his lap, saying: "You're comfortable there, I trust."

Tristan nodded.

"Then let's begin. First, a question I'd like answered: "Why did your father have your medical papers destroyed...? Do you know?"

"Yes," Tristan stated plainly. "It was my father's conviction that no one should ever be -- exposed to me in any way. He was certain they'd go mad."

Knapp wrote for a minute, then asked: "Is that why you became a recluse? To honor your father's wishes?"

"Well, maybe he was right, because both my parents did die insane, as they'd always feared."

"What happened to them?"

Tristan thought about his mother's sweet face, her smile, remembering watching her work.

"Yellow jack..." Tristan replied. "We had an epidemic in nineteen-ought-five, five years ago. My mother, Dolores, was an illustrator for magazines and newspapers. Very popular she was, but -- she had fits, hallucinations... She never recovered, never returned to reality. And she... died of fright in Charity Hospital a year later."

He recalled the image of her struggling to escape the orderlies' grasp, their carrying her bodily into her room, and shutting the door on him.

"So you say they knew... they would end their days in madness? Each of them?"

Tristan said: "Yes, both."

"Did they tell you that?"

"Many times."

From the end table beside him, Knapp picked up a small, framed lithograph of a tall, balding, red-faced, thick-necked man with mutton chop whiskers, with an implacable glower belying a dignified pose.

"How did they say it -- to you?"

"My father, M'sieur Étienne, -- He was terribly frustrated with me. He'd say it in anger -- that someday I shall drive him mad...! My mother, when deep in despair... "

"Tell me more about your father."

"Upon my mother's death, he tried to kill me."

Knapp reacted with suppressed outrage.

The young man relived the memory of his being strangled in deadly earnest, detailing the scene vividly, and how Nicholas sprang into action, pulling his Master away from his son, and grappling till he achieved the advantage, pushing the maddened printer headfirst into a wall, knocking him out.

"He tried to throttle me! His only son. Right here in the parlor. *I* was to blame, he said -- he *insisted! 'You're to blame!'* That's when Nicholas came in and subdued him quickly. He saved my life. Then he bound my father's hands and feet with the cord from the portiere and telephoned the police. While I stood by... "

" -- trying to recover from this assault, yes?"

"Yes, I was badly shaken."

"I've no doubt!"

"My father was tried and declared insane."

He remembered the thin, elderly, bearded judge who presided over the case.

"The judge sent him to the Touro Infirmary. To a padded cell. A few days later, he feigned illness, overpowered an orderly in his cell, and bashed his own brains in with the heel of the man's shoe."

Knapp exhaled heavily. "Is that even possible?"

"Anything's possible to the insane, Professor. You know it's true."

"Or so they think...!"

For the time being, Knapp was at a loss for more words, stirring in his seat, sublimating his emotions and trying to phrase his next question.

Meantime, Tristan continued: "Now it's five years later, and I want to forget... and I know I can't do it alone... But right now, I don't think I can say anymore... Do you mind if that's all for today? Please... "

Knapp took a breath.

"Ask Nicholas for some luncheon. You must be hungry."

"Are you sure you've done enough? Maybe if you just relax a while. Otherwise it's a rather brief session."

Tristan seems speechless; his eyes brim with fresh tears.

"Very well," Knapp conceded. "I'll go."

He couldn't subdue the feeling of pity he held for Tristan, but exited the parlor without further comment.

Nicholas intercepted him on his way to the foyer.

"M'sieur, do you mind if I suggest your taking our buckboard back to the Carrollton?"

"No, I don't mind. You'll take me there and back?"

"Actually, Miss Anne Adele was hoping to accompany you and return it herself. She thought the family carriage unnecessary."

"I see. Will she be ready to leave soon?"

"She is waiting outdoors, m'sieur."

He opened the front door, flooding the foyer with sunlight.

On the porch, Anne Adele, dressed quite smartly with sunbonnet and pastel-hued parasol, turned to face Professor Knapp. The small conveyance and team stood by.

"Ah, yes, thank you," he smiled, dismissing Nicholas.

The rich orange sun shone just above the treetops.

"Good day, Professor."

"Miss Anne Adele."

30

"You may call me simply 'Anne'."

"So I shall... I understand we are leaving together?"

They walked the several yards to the waiting carriage, Knapp already enjoying her company.

"I hope you don't mind. I have some errands to run in town."

"Not at all... It's very convenient, in fact, as I need to talk to you in private."

"I thought you might."

"To be blunt, I must say I find it... most unlikely that neither you nor Nicholas share Tristan's secret."

"But I assure you that I do *not* know, and in fact, I've never *wanted* to know."

"'Never wanted to'?"

"Not since I reached the age of reason."

"Not even now?"

"He'll tell me his secret if he ever wants to. And I'll help him any way I can, but... I don't wish to go mad myself as a result."

Her face betrayed guilt, he saw clearly. Reaching the post, he loosened the reins.

"I see. There was never any kind of jealousy between you, was there?"

"I never felt any. In fact, when we were little, we played in secret. We were supervised most of the time, but children *will* disobey. I was a high-spirited girl."

With a mutual smile, they climbed up onto the buckboard and sat; he took up the reins.

"So you took pity on your little – on Tristan. When did you leave home?"

"I was twenty. Father never forgave me, of course... Anything else you -- need to ask?"

Knapp mentally nudged away an errant thought about Celia and answered: "I always have more questions. Some could be more or less distressing."

"Try me!" she unexpectedly beamed.

"Here," thought the psychologist, "is a modern woman!"

"What became of your own mother?"

"She died bearing me... I've known about it for many years. Father told me but ironically, I suppose, he never seemed to blame me --"

" -- as Tristan was blamed for his mother's madness."

"Yes... So odd... Is there anything else?"

Their eyes met; hers were a paler blue than his, he noticed.

"Not right now." Knapp mumbled, settling himself, ready to travel, gathering the reins' slack.

Anne Adele smiled to herself inscrutably.

That instant, a sharp, not-too-distant moan alarmed them both. And then the piercing wail of what almost sounded like a dying kitten or infant!

"*What* in God's Name is *that?!*" Knapp shouted.

Anne Adele remained seated as Knapp leapt from the carriage, over to and up the steps, and back inside Maison Duquesne, rushing past Nicholas.

"Where are you going, Professor?" inquired the butler with growing alarm. "What are you doing...? I must announce you, m'sieur!"

But Knapp was ascending the stairs two at a time.

***

Chapter Six

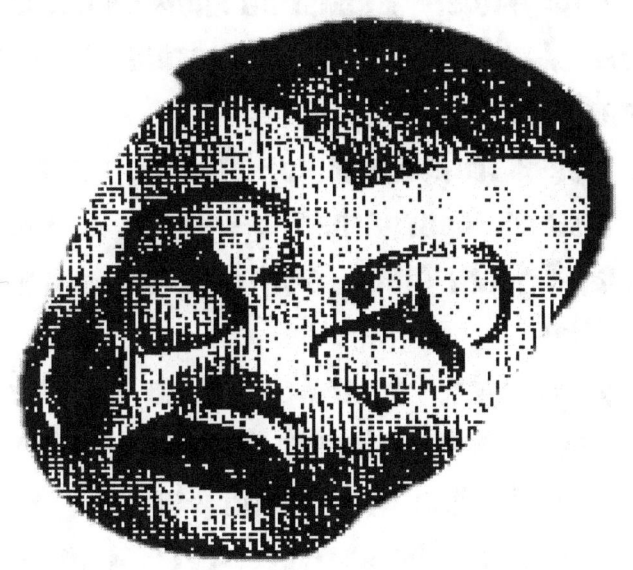

Intrusions

Knapp pushed open the upstairs parlor doors and entered boldly. He'd endured enough obstruction, enough mystery, and wanted explanations *now!*

He saw the room was empty, but the adjoining door to the master bedroom ajar.

"Tristan, could you come out of your bedroom, please? There's a matter we must discuss *immediately!*"

Tristan timidly edged around the doorway into the room, stopping at the window as before.

"What was that sound I heard? -- Tristan, you can't allow me to work in the dark this way."

"Perhaps darkness is better," Tristan lowed.

"Twaddle! Don't take steps backward! You must tell me your secret – *now.*"

"It's too soon! Trust me!"

"How can I? Impossible. I insist on knowing before I leave these rooms again. And *if I leave, I will not return.* According to our agreement."

"Please! I can't!"

"No hood can hide a troubled mind, Tristan, my boy. I can't *guess* my way into yours... "He slowly approached. "Tell me. Take off the hood."

Nearing trauma, Tristan sidled swiftly away, crying: "No! Impossible! You'd get sick! And die!"

Pursuing, Knapp pressed: "What d'you mean by that? Why would I die?"

"I should have known better than to trust my soul to a stranger!"

"You won't trust me? You won't confide in me? As a friend?"

*"It's – not – yet – time!"*he shrieked, yet not the same one, Knapp was aware.

The professor sighed: "Then the time has come for me to take my permanent leave."

He turned on his heel to exit the parlor, and nearly collided with Nicholas and Anne Adele, rushing to comfort their loved one before his tantrum escalated.

"Knapp, you wretch! You wretched bastard!" tormented Tristan raged. "I knew you'd bring it to this! Too fast! Too far, too fast...! Lying, unfeeling bastard!"

Anne Adele fought the urge to embrace him, only saying: "It's all right, Tristan."

Nicholas, brow tight with concern, brought his disconsolate master gushing self-pitying tears, to his chair.

Knapp stood just outside the parlor in the hallway, listening and forcing emotional detachment as Tristan carried on. Anne Adele emerged, confronting him coldly.

"Why have you upset him like this?"

"What what's that cry? That wasn't his voice."

"What do you mean? Of course it was! Who else --?"

"I'm weary of secrets." Knapp began to descend the staircase. "I shall need my hat and coat, my gloves."

"Come back here!" she demanded. "You can't leave now!"

By then, Nicholas had joined Miss Anne Adele at the top of the stairs. They exchanged worried looks and hurried down after their departing guest.

Tristan sat on the edge of his bed, facing the hallway door, still beside himself with grief.

"It's – not fair! Why was he so impatient?! Oh, I'm a damned fool...!"

Slowly, the door swung open, pushed stealthily from the other side by a long, dappled hand.

Tristan froze in panic.

There stood another stranger, a very strange stranger indeed. Flamboyantly attired in a rainbow-splotched smock, a gaunt, mustachioed character, ominously quiet as he revealed himself fully, scrutinizing Tristan closely.

The hooded young man slid himself backward across the bed's expanse, panting in terror.

"M'syoor Duquesne...?"

Dumbstruck, Tristan recoiled off the bedside, clutching the bedpost for support, and back against the nearest wall.

"I am Thorndike, the artist! Undoubtedly you wonder what I am doing here in your private chambers. I will explain honestly, for I have nothing to hide, you see. I admit curiosity brought me here, but now that I see who and what you are, I am puzzled, utterly perplexed! You are no gargoyle...!" the Bohemian overplayed, for now he felt the need to force more inspiration forward.

35

"Your face, in fact, bears such nobility that I am even more inspired to paint or sculpt it than before! My dear Duquesne, such a face should not be hidden from view! Will you sit for me, sir? I must immortalize that face!"

Tristan's fear gave way to righteous anger. He pointed to the door with a quavering finger.

"Get out of this room! Out of this house! *Go!*"

"But, m'syoor! All of New Orleans awaits your arrival! The Mardi Gras beckons! We might even elect you "Rex"!"

Nicholas entered at last, icy indignation intensifying his brisk actions; he collared the eccentric intruder and pulled him out into the hallway.

Still, Thorndike roared: "You're too late, my good man! Your so-called monster has been unmasked! And he must share his face with the world!"

"How dare you invade our privacy! Get out of here fast, I say, and never show your face 'round here again!"

The Creole virtually hurled him down the stairs.

At the bottom waited a surprised Knapp and Anne Adele. Thorndike landed clumsily, almost going over the bannister, which stopped his rapid descent.

"Aha, the businessman! My friend, I've seen the Medusa! And lived!"

Nicholas stumped down the stairs, caught and propelled the headstrong artist down the remaining steps, through the foyer, and sailing off the porch. The trespasser landed on his face, next to his tethered horse.

The servant slammed the front door, then turned and, glowering at Knapp as he passed, hurried back upstairs, following closely, yet Knapp and Anne Adele could hear the madman continue to rant: "This doesn't stop me! Not I, Gilbert Thorndike! I remain undaunted, do you hear me?! This doesn't stop me...!"

The three reached the parlor together, and saw the bedroom door closed. Nicholas spoke to the one beyond it. "He is gone, m'sieur. Such a crazy man should never have been able to enter the house if I were doing my job properly..."

Knapp felt moved to apologize as well. "This is my fault, Tristan. It wouldn't have happened if I'd known that hooligan was here."

There was a lull before Anne Adele said: "Tristan?"

Next moment, Tristan opened the door and stepped out into the parlor. All instantly noticed that he'd seemed to have calmed himself considerably, though still unnerved a bit.

Knapp resisted displaying, as the others did not, a mild surprise, and, feeling obliged to continue, explained: "I'm sorry, Tristan. The man's a raving lunatic. We met at Bégué's. I should never have spoken to him in the first place..."

"No apologies necessary, Knapp, m'good fellow," smiled Tristan wanly.

This time all reacted with genuine, spontaneous, delighted wonderment.

"This outrageous intrusion just now has -- strengthened me somehow... I was taken by surprise, forced to deal with the man myself, and out of necessity, met the challenge..."

"Bravo, m'sieur!" cheered Nicholas.

"Oh, my poor baby brother!" Anne Adele exhaled with great relief.

"And I ordered him out! Me, myself...! And do you know what? Meeting even the likes of him wasn't quite as bad as I had imagined!"

"Your need outfought your fear, Tristan," Professor Knapp smiled.

"Perhaps it was for the best, after all," Nicholas nodded.

"It was. It *was...!*" Tristan quaked with excitement. "I was wrong, Knapp. I realize now that I must keep challenging myself in order to conquer my fear, over and over again, if I have faith enough... that I can."

Knapp seized the opportunity. "Then, you're *ready...?*"

Tristan nodded gravely and retreated into his master bedroom. Knapp handed his journal to Nicholas.

"Keep this downstairs for me. I won't need it till later. Thank you." To Anne he said: "I'm sorry if I seemed cruel before. I had to *know...* D'you understand?"

37

She took his hand instinctively. "Yes." Then she let go, more mindful of her actions.

Knapp entered the bedroom...

Tristan sat waiting at bedside, clasping his hands tightly as Knapp entered and closed the door behind them. He sighed as the older man drew nearer.

"This will be for the best, I'm sure of it," Knapp said.

"I wish I were... Where are Anne Adele and Nicholas?"

"Do you want them here?"

"No, I love them too much to show them this... Well, we'd better get on with it. I don't know how long my courage will last."

"Very well then... I'm ready if you are."

Tristan looked up at Knapp pleadingly, as if silently asking forgiveness before committing a grievous sin. Then he slowly pulled the hood back, letting it gather at his shoulders. His dark hair is long, thin, unkempt, matted.

"Go 'round the other side..."

Knapp circumvented the bed corner, facing his back, watching as he made his way... His eyes widened with horror. He became nauseous but contained himself as best he could from expressing complete revulsion, and yet he could not look away!

He saw that on the back of Tristan's head there was another face nestled in the long, damp hair.

It was the face of a hideous, childlike twin, blind and mute, with a ghastly pallor and complexion. The Face squinted and ogled and drooled incontinently, aware somehow of its liberation from darkness.

Tristan sighed again; his shoulders slumped and he tilted his head to one side. The Face now seemed to be looking curiously about, as if alert to Knapp's presence.

Knapp, staring in awed disbelief, forced himself to blink to clear the panic from his eyes. His hand rose to clutch his breast, as the repulsive, cretinous face grew momentarily excited. It uttered infantile noises in a puling moan of a voice that grated the nerves of both men visibly. Then the weird visage becalmed itself.

Tristan was on the edge of more miserable tears, though his shame and discomfort belied a trembling glimmer of hope.

Knapp, still transfixed, took a little time to catch his breath and bring himself back under control.

Without moving, Knapp asked: "Does it *see?*"

"No..."

"Does it speak?"

"No."

"Does it... sleep?"

"Yes, when I sleep... When I'm awake, it makes horrible sounds sometimes, like the crying you heard. Frequently. Faithfully."

Knapp wanted to look away, but didn't. "'Crying'? What about --?"

"Shall I replace the hood?"

"No, no. That won't do... Not yet. I'm not finished with the examination... It does take some getting used to."

"I can vouch for that...! At least I don't have to look at it much... if I don't want to... use a mirror. You were going to ask another question -- ?"

"Does it laugh? -- No, eat. Does it eat? I can see that he breathes."

"It shares my throat. But no, it doesn't take food... It breathes, it sleeps, laughs idiotically from time to time. It cries,,, and it's slowly driving me insane."

"I -- couldn't imagine bearing this burden myself, Tristan... You must possess enormous inner strength."

Tristan snorted: "It's a parasite, my ingrown twin. All the bawling and bleating and wailing and the moaning and giggling -- Oh, yes, it has quite a rich sense of humor! And the drooling and the sniffing and -- the *knowing, my* knowing that it's *there...!* Always there..."

Professor Knapp averted his eyes, and saw a colorful feather wedged between the mattress and the bedpost. He collected and fingered it distractedly while listening.

"I can't escape it, Knapp. It has a mind of its own, though not much of one..."

He turned a bit in Knapp's direction, reclaiming his fullest attention.

"Yes, go on."

""I can't even lie flat on my back. I might suffocate it — my mad brother."

Knapp made a mental note of that phrase.

"And maybe myself, if the windpipe is closed. So the doctor said. And so I must always sleep on my side. That is, if it *allows* me to sleep!"

"It's a wonder you're *not* mad, really."

They shared a glance at each other.

"*Aren't* I, Knapp? I'm counting on your word for it."

"Don't talk nonsense... He doesn't think, then? Although you share a brain?"

"It shares *my* brain. I do the real thinking, thank God."

"Yes... Now, then, is it 'driving you insane'?"

"With ease, Knapp...!" he smiled wearily.

Knapp continued battling his emotions as he observed the monstrous Face once again, placing the feather in his waistcoat pocket while practicing self-control.

"It rolls its eyes. — *That* I can feel. It screams when it's threatened, or even touched! That awful, piping shriek, like a banshee! It laughs and cries for no reason at the most unwanted times, and sometimes it prattles on and on in its own lunatic language for hours on end... It's a curse."

"Don't be melodramatic. A curse could only work if you believe in it," Knapp defended.

He dared to lean in and look more closely while Tristan extended his deepest thoughts.

40

The mouth of the Face was open wider now, seemingly trying to bite or perhaps say something. The nostrils flared, eyes showing only white.

"Knapp, I can't even bear to see this face anymore! And I *haven't* seen it since before my parents died. I promised myself that. I have stayed in this house not just since then, but since the age of three, alone in my room most of my life, ... sleeping alone... Father discouraged everyone from entering here."

Knapp interrupted, softly suggesting: "Tristan, I'd like to take a closer look and probe a bit with my finger, unless you prefer I don't..."

Tristan, wrestling his emotions, didn't answer.

"Just try to relax..."

Knapp raised his hand, index finger extended, and cautiously prepared to touch the nightmarish countenance.

A closer look revealed that the Face was a smaller, cruder version of Tristan, overgrown with the master twin's hair blending into a thin beard of its own, two normal-sized eyes, a short, snoutlike nose, and two tiny ears crushed behind larger ones.

His fingertip came within touching distance. The Face knew it was there; the jaws and tongue moved; the blind eyes searched; the squat nose twitched.

Knapp touched the pimply cheek gingerly. The Face squealed and gibbered with sudden force and rolled the eyes in primitive panic. Knapp's hand recoiled in instinctive terror.

Then he noticed something under the gathers of the hood. His finger probed to reveal something like a thin, white collar down there. Pulling it back further revealed tubing connected to the apparatus's underside.

"What's this?"

"That is its trough," Tristan sighed. "It was designed and built by Doctor Perrault to collect the rather steady stream of saliva it oozes... There's a drainage sac attached just below. Ingenious, isn't it?"

"Necessary as well."

A feeble snort, then: "I'm afraid so..."

41

Knapp refocused on the Face itself. He tapped the nose with his finger, then brushed it with the feather from his pocket. The Face slobbered and sniffed and, with a seeming smile, settled into a regular, dormant breathing pattern.

Knapp tucked the feather back in his pocket; then his fingers gently found the edge of the hood and replaced it, careful not to disturb its contents.

Then he stood erect and walked back around the bed to face Tristan anew. Each waited for the other to speak first...

"Are you thoroughly disgusted now?" asked Master Tristan.

Knapp considered his words with care: "Surgery might help. Was it ever discussed? Have you ever thought about it?"

"Doctor Perrault did, at one time. But he decided it would be too risky. I might *also* be -- removed."

"Imperiling your brain in so doing, you mean."

"Yes. Plus, my parents could never decide."

"I see, but, -- Well, why don't we consult with my medical friends in Boston? Perhaps the advances being made -- "

"No, all they'd be able to do is cover it up, simply disguise what will always be there." He stood, speaking with intensity: "Knapp, make me a promise. You must tell *no one, especially not Anne Adele nor Nicholas* what you have just seen... Promise me, Knapp!"

Knapp crossed to the dresser and saw himself in its cloudy, dark-edged mirror, along with an expectant Tristan behind him. He turned, leaning back against the furniture.

"I agree... But I must add that to continue to ignore this -- 'affliction' by denying it and hiding it from the world can only bring you more unhappiness."

"*Ignore* it?! It is impossible to ignore!"

"May I remind you that you once thought it was impossible for *anyone* to know your secret and remain sane... but I saw it, and I'm not about to lose my sanity over it! And neither would Anne Adele or Nicholas, who know you

42

better...! How is it that they don't know anything about this? How could they not know? Or guess?"

"I don't know what they might know... " Tristan hung his head glumly. "They've never seen... never asked."

"But the noises, the –?"

Tristan suddenly slammed himself back up against the open, waiting wall! *"They've never asked, I said!"*

Knapp remained unflappable. "Why not...? Breathe deeply."

Tristan followed his advice and felt better in seconds.

"Nicholas – because he feels it's not his place to question the master of the house – "

"Of course."

"Anne Adele, because – I don't know, really... Because she was told never to ask! I suppose they think *I* make all that noise!"

"*I* wouldn't..."

"But now you've promised not to tell them, Knapp. You've got to keep your promise."

"I will, Tristan," nodded Knapp. "But *you've* got to promise *yourself* to continue to be brave – brave enough to *want* to show them your so-called 'mad brother', *soon* perhaps, and learn to stop living in dread... Stop being a martyr to it... You must learn to *accept* your strange fate, and try to live as happy and – normal a life as you can..."

Tristan stepped away from his wall, regarding him with wordless gratitude.

Knapp smiled back. "Now, by your leave, I will go downstairs and make note of our progress in my journal... Meantime, you think over what I've said."

Tristan had a brainstorm: "Knapp! I want you to stay... "

"You may join me downstairs if you like."

"No, I mean I want you to stay here at Maison Duquesne for the duration of my treatment."

Taken aback, Knapp crowed: "What? More progress? Remarkable...!

43

I'll stay as long as I'm needed. At least overnight, in case you want to talk some more," he smiled openly. Then, tasking his hand: "Thank you... more for your courage and trust than for your hospitality."

"Knapp," Tristan confessed, "I feel like crying again."

"You should be laughing, not crying!" He let go of his hand to wag an admonishing finger. "You cry too much. I'm surprised they don't think you're peeling onions up here!"

Tristan laughed, to his own surprise.

"That's what Doctor Freud would say!" Knapp joked, eliciting more unexpected laughter.

"Why, look at me, Knapp! It's the first time I've laughed in years!"

"You should read Mark Twain. Or follow politics... Oh, by the way, -- " He found the feather again. "I found this on the floor just now... From your pillow?"

"No... Let me show you something else."

Tristan took the feather, circumambulated to the foot of his bed, lifted the edge of the mattress, and extracted the *gris-gris* ball. He stuck the feather in it and showed it closely to Knapp.

"What in the world is that?"

"It's called a *gris-gris.* It's a voodoo charm. Nicholas puts one there every week. I'm not supposed to know about it, of course, or it won't work. That's the custom. Usually, when he changes linens, he just puts it there for good luck, and replaces it with a fresh one..."

He handed the ball to Knapp, who turned it over hand-to-hand, careful not to dislodge its feathers.

"A little charade we play. I wish he would mention it sometime. I'm bored with hiding his secret for him."

"That's a good sign."

"Is it --?"

"Think about it, what you just said."

44

"Yes, I see what you're steering for. Keeping secrets takes its toll."

"You know it first-hand."

"Yes... " Tristan distracted himself with the action of taking back the trinket.

"Want to know what it's made of? Just some old, dried manure and spices, really. 'And magic!" the natives would say."

"Ah, yes. I imagine that they would."

"It's a very specific recipe, a lady servant told me once. The feathers are for decoration only. The native boys cook them up for the old witch-queen. They're meant to attract kindly spirits and help me survive."

"Well, then, -- " Knapp took back the charm and replaced it under the mattress. "I hope it does the job."

"I think it's already started. Couldn't you smell it?"

Now Knapp enjoyed an unanticipated burst of laughter as, almost embarrassedly, Tristan laughed along with him, his newfound elation overcoming his usual anxiety.

Meantime, in the hallway, Anne Adele and Nicholas appeared together from different rooms and looked at each in surprise. Was that laughter from within those closed doors..?!

"I'm glad you laughed, Knapp. I don't make many jokes."

The Professor headed for the door to the hallway.

"Will you be gone long, Knapp?" Tristan asked anxiously. "And will you be staying?"

Knapp stopped. "Tristan, I understand your reluctance to let me go just now... Do *you*?"

The young man considered a moment, then nodded affirmatively.

"You trust me. You just proved it. I promise to not only keep your secret, but to help you live as full a life as you desire. And as you proved with that ass Thorndike, no obstacle, human or otherwise, should deter you along your way."

45

Knapp opened the door. Anne Adele and Nicholas were there, waiting expectantly, happily. Smiling, Tristan stepped closer to them.

"Please... Come in!" he beckoned.

His loved ones shone with incredulous smiles and joyous tears. Anne Adele gripped Tristan's hands firmly; the two laughed nervously together as Nicholas filled with happiness and a touch of pride for his part in it.

Knapp stepped out into the hallway and proceeded downstairs, still able to hear the conversation above.

"Did I hear you laugh?!"

"Yes, Anne, you did! And soon, I'll even dare to walk outside in the sun!"

Knapp indulged himself in a small smile of satisfaction.

***

Chapter Seven

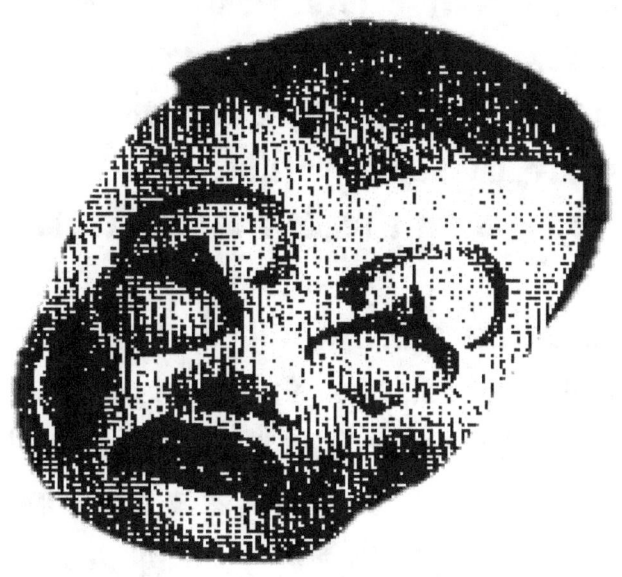

Progress

With one sweep, Knapp pulled open the ponderous maroon drape. The flood of sunshine that burst through into the downstairs parlor made Tristan recoil and shade his eyes as he sat upon the sofa.

"Is that really necessary, Knapp?"

"I think so..." He went to the desk where his journal lay open, sat and took pen in hand. "Now why don't you lie down while we talk?"

"Why should I? I've only been awake -- "

"Because I don't want you pacing up and down the walls and running out the door...!" he chided, then smiled: "Relax. We'll be here awhile. Lie back on the sofa."

"On my side, you mean."

"However you're comfortable. Don't nit-pick."

Tristan reclined uneasily, then adjusted himself so he could see Knapp, who noticed it.

"No, no, the way you were before, please."

The young Duquesne sat up again, puzzled.

"It may help you not to see me while you talk."

He resumed his original supine position.

"It couldn't be that you don't really trust me, could it?"

"No..."

"Good. Because I trust *you*... We'll be fine as long as we don't fall asleep. My name may be Knapp, but don't you dare take one."

"I'm not *paying* for these jokes, am I?" Tristan mocked archly.

"Very good! But a word of advice: Never be funnier than the teacher."

Tristan chuckled, relaxing a bit more, Knapp observed.

"Now, I'd like to hear more about your parents. Anything you care to say."

Tensing a touch, the young man began: "Well, as I said before, Father was a printer by trade, a professional man, and exacting by nature. He suffered no fools. Had a dozen shops in all, two in New Orleans."

Knapp wrote down all of it.

"After the third shop opened is when he had the telephone installed, I remember... How proud and excited he was! Showed how it works to Mother and we children. Anne Adele seemed bored, I recall, but I was excited too, and Mother was... well, tolerant, at least. Once she tried to use it and Father grew very impatient with her ignorance and shouted great obscenities at her, or words I couldn't understand, at least. I was watching from behind a portière..."

"I'm listening..." Knapp reassured.

"He... printed trade cards and the like for local stores and other businesses. He got rich with his chromolithographs. As for Mother,

48

Father hired her as an illustrator. Seventeen years his junior she was... And soon they were wed, in eighteen-eighty-three. Doctor Perrault was best man... Anne Adele told me it was a lovely ceremony."

"Did Anne Adele ever relate her outside experiences to you?"

"Yes, quite often. She was the child of Father's first marriage, of course. He never talked about it, at least never to me... I remember watching her and her playmates cavorting under the willows, from right there." He pointed toward the window.

"What else about your stepsister?"

"She told me her own mother died on the operating table. I suppose I'm lucky by comparison... I *knew my* mother, and she was... beautiful, before – "

"Go on. Before what?"

"She changed – grew apart from us, little by little. At first, she would take me to her easel and show me how she drew the willow tree, for instance, and I watched, and learned, though I know I didn't evidence any similar talent. I was very young then. I remember running back and forth from the easel to the window, comparing it to the tree outside, to feel part of her work, I suppose."

"How did she change?"

"She fell prone to fits. Fits of despair. Once when my hood got loose as I played on the floor, she just dropped her charcoal pencil, buried her face in her hands and wept, softly but... deeply. That made me cry too. I couldn't understand... "

"Loved ones leave us in different ways sometimes..."

"I see what you mean, Knapp," Tristan reflected. "The day she left our house – "

"Yes? Tell me about that."

"She was – trying to come downstairs, but stopped on the staircase halfway down, stricken by something, some thought perhaps, that rooted her to the spot. She was swaying, dangerously, seemed to be hallucinating. I was

49

scared. I screamed, I think. Nicholas came down and went to her aid, and I
--!"

Knapp and Tristan sat upright in unison, the latter electrified with self-discovery.

"Knapp! I just realized something! I just recalled -- that day, the day Mother was taken to Charity Hospital, I panicked -- saw her on the stairs -- couldn't move forward to be at her side -- I went *backward!* Knapp! The *wall!* I flew back against the wall!"

Knapp set down his pen.   "Significant, to be sure, Tristan. Yes. And now it remains for us to do something about it!"

That night, at the desk under the wedding portrait of Étienne and Dolores, Knapp, in his shirtsleeves, studied his notes from that day's session by candlelight, reading back:
"Why do you call that Face the 'mad brother'?"
"Because he *is* mad, and because he wants to drive *me* mad as well."
"How could a madman make a decision like that?"
"He knows..."
"But how do *you* know? Does he have thoughts? Can you read his mind?"
"No, it keeps whatever thoughts it may have to itself. But sometimes I think he's reading mine... Oh, I don't know. Maybe he doesn't think after all."
A separate note to himself: "T began to refer to Face as "he" not "it." Not sure that's good. Try different approach tomorrow."
"Of course not... Then it's all mere assumption on your part, isn't it?"
"Is it...? Yes, you're right. It's pretty childish of me to call him that."
Then Knapp stopped reading and wrote: "On this, our second day of formal sessions, T has already begun to abandon his belief that his vengeful "mad brother" is persecuting him. "Frater Dementis" is the term I've chosen to describe this particular form of schizophrenia. T called it a parasite, a curse.

50

I must help him redirect his way of thinking about it."

Knapp extinguished the candle and retired.

Next morning, at the start of their third session, Knapp, pen in hand at his journal, asked the reclining Tristan: "Have you ever felt any kind of influence the Face may be trying to exert upon you... in any way?"

"Make me do things...? No, I am Master here."

"Then you've never experienced, or received any intelligent thoughts or feelings generated by it, no matter how trivial, or primitive? No -- overwhelming urges?"

"No, never... None that weren't my own. Although I used to thi-- "

Suddenly, a shrill, strained tittering arose in Tristan's throat, though not issued through his mouth. He sat bolt upright, clutching tightly at his gullet, eyes wide.

"Good Lord!" Knapp barked involuntarily. He stood, leaning with both fists on the desk until the weird laughter subsided.

"You see, Knapp? He *knows!*" The tortured young man stood and shook his fists. "He knows I'm talking about him!"

"Sit down! *Sit down this instant!*"

Tristan sat, tried to control himself.

"Did you hear what you just said? You said 'he'. What nonsense! It is not thinking being. You know that. It's a part of you, yes, an extra part that did not develop, and not a pleasant thing to live with, *but live with it you must, and cope with it you must...*"

Tristan buried his face in his hands.

"Are you crying again?"

"No, it's only that -- I'm sorry. I was just embarrassed."

"Of course... Well, I don't blame you for that. However, you should learn to *expect* it in the company of others, and expect them to *understand*. And they will... It's distracting enough without *your* carrying on."

"I'm sorry."

"I forgive you. Just think first, next time... Now relax awhile. I'd like to make some notes."

Tristan Duquesne sighed deeply and sat back as Knapp wrote.

In the large, exquisite but shadowy dining room, Miss Duquesne and Professor Knapp sat opposite each other at the vast table, Tristan at the head.

"So, Miss Anne Adele, what errands have you been running in the city?" inquired Knapp halfway through their meal of capon, Creole style, yams, greens and biscuits.

"Nothing of a personal nature. I'm involved in Father's business, in case you weren't aware."

"No, I wasn't."

"She moved to Baltimore several years ago to oversee one of our busiest shops there," remarked Tristan, chewing.

"Don't speak with your mouth full," she admonished.

"Interesting," plumbed Knapp. "Someone -- a young lady I know -- is also a shopkeeper."

"I don't manage the shop, Professor. I simply write the checks and make sure the books are balanced once a month."

"I see... By the way, 'Professor's a bit formal, isn't it? My friends call me Bill."

"And 'Bill' is quite *in*formal," she teased. "I'd prefer to call you William. I've always liked that name."

"Then by all means, call me William."

She smiled at Knapp, who smiled back, then at Tristan, who smiled back politely.

Another night passed, uneventfully. All slept well.

Knapp yanked the heavy curtain open, now an opening ritual. They took their positions and commenced.

"How did you experiment with it? How did you try to make contact?"

"Little ways..."

"Such as --? I'll make it easy for you. I'll mention some forms of physical stimuli, and all you need do is tell me if you've ever felt the Face register any sort of reaction to it. And how it reacted, good or bad. Want to try it?"

"All right."

"Ready? -- Fire."

"Oh, he doesn't like that!"

"Cold?"

"It surprises him. That's all."

"A pinch or a slap?"

"He doesn't seem to mind, doesn't understand."

"Naturally not. -- Water?"

"I'm careful not to expose the Face to it for any length of time. Doctor Perrault warned that if he drowned, I would too."

"It's logical you'd suffer a number of things together. Now don't be embarrassed to tell me -- How does it react to masturbation?"

"That is a vice in which I rarely indulge. Mother discouraged it strongly. I've never noticed any sensual interest in him."

"It seems you were prevented from experiencing almost everything in life without guilt... When you were a child, did you resent -- ?"

"'Resent'?! I hated him! Hated him...! Can't you imagine what it's like to be hated yourself?! Hidden, shunned by all, having no one to play with or even talk to, my own age?! I despised him for that and I still do!"

Beside himself, Tristan got up, went to a small table with a porcelain figure of an old riverboat captain, smashed the knickknack to the floor and clutched the window drape to his face.

"*Whom* do you despise? Who prevented you from -- ?"

"My brother! My damned mad brother! Who else did you think I meant, my fa-- ?"

An epiphany of self-realization brought a trembling hand to his lips.

Knapp walked over to him, set a hand on his shoulder.

"Yes. Who else indeed, Tristan? *Who* shunned you and feared you and kept you a virtual prisoner in his house? *Who* made those feelings known?"

The young man, struggling internally, collapsed into tears.

"Oh, dear God! Father, ... Why wouldn't you share the sunlight...?"

Knapp guided him back to the sofa and reseated himself, watching as Tristan calmed himself before continuing.

"I'm going to bring up a painful memory now, Tristan. Prepare yourself... You say your father tried to kill you -- "

"He did. He was on the telephone, I remember, with one of his shops, and I was watching him, that's all. Just watching him. I came into the parlor and stood there, next to a portière. He watched me come in, talked a little more, then hung up the earpiece, and then the next instant -- he was at my throat."

"What did he say? Anything?"

"He said *I* killed her! Drove her insane and killed her!"

"Your mother."

"Yes."

"You'd done nothing to provoke his anger that day?"

"Nothing. Ever."

"But her death was the work of the yellow jack, wasn't it?"

"That's what Doctor Perrault told us. But she was also -- going mad, it seemed. She frightened easily."

"And yet he blamed you, not her sickness?"

"Yes, and that was -- "

"Was what?

"-- terribly unfair of him, wasn't it?"

"You have just said it."

"Mother always loved me... even after she'd forgotten me... She'd hold me... She never cared that I had another face. She loved *me!*"

"Of course. It's very natural for a mother to love her son."

Later, Knapp wrote: "Progress has been made thus far, albeit slowly. Tristan has admitted hating and resenting his father, whose meieval family ethic has left cruel psychological scars deep within his son, intentionally or not. If this were ancient Sparta, I'm certain Étienne would have left his son on a mountaintop to die." He scratched out the last sentence, glanced aimlessly around the room, then wrote: "On the subject of T's therapy, I've just had an idea that I believe will work."

***

Chapter Eight

More Progress

Tristan was bored, but continued the tiresome exercise as instructed. The daylight from outside hurt his eyes less with each session, he realized.

Knapp simply sat and observed him standing with his back to the wall, slowly walk forward to the center of the room, return to the wall and repeat the action. He wrote: "Today I initiated a simple exercise to combat his unique condition of "muromania" (staying close to walls to avoid any curiosity about the back of his head). I shall have him practice this therapy of walking away from walls repeatedly in order for him to learn to control that regressive urge."

Anne Adele joined them and sat on the window-seat, sharing encouraging smiles and nods with Tristan as she watched.

"The very tedium of this effort may, I hope, at length produce the result of his gaining independence, and confidence in himself and in others," Knapp continued. "Yet progress is slow... I've got to bring him *outdoors* soon. But how to approach him about it?"

Looking at Anne Adele, he formulated a plan...

She was in the drawing room next morning, sifting through Dolores's tablet of sketches. A gentle knock stirred her.

"Good morning, Miss Duquesne," greeted Knapp, entering.

"Good morning. Come in, please."

"I didn't see you at breakfast."

"I was up earlier than you men, William. I fixed myself something. I do it all the time at home, in Baltimore. I live alone, you know."

"Er, yes... I must say this is a very elegant room."

"Mother's drawing room it was. I was just looking at some of her old sketches. Care to see some?"

He took one. "Why, that's quite good! Lovely..."

Their eyes met.

"The fact is I have a favor to ask you."

She set the tablet aside.

"For Tristan..."

A short while later, Knapp entered the sunny downstairs parlor and opened his journal. Tristan was already on the sofa.

"I hope you won't mind, but I'd like to shorten our morning session today. To about an hour."

"Why?"

"Miss Anne and I would like to take the carriage for a tour of your Garden District. Forgive me, but I've been feeling rather confined these past few days."

"Oh... Yes, I see."

"We won't be gone long. And we can resume our work when I return...
You *don't* mind, do you?"

"No, of course not. Anne Adele is good company. She claims to be quite
shy about men, but seems -- "

Abruptly, he gagged; his hands went to his throat. A steady stream of
gibberish was coming from beneath Tristan's hood. The Voice was soft,
childlike, but piercing. Tristan gripped the cushion beneath him until it lessened
by degrees.

Knapp scrutinized him closely, despite having to wince himself at the very
unnerving nature of these sounds.

Finally, the weird interlude passed. Tristan relaxed wearily, trying to
subdue his mortification as fast as possible.

"Shall we begin again?" Knapp asked.

"I'm ready," he rasped. Then, clearing his throat, reiterated: "I'm ready."

"What about Anne Adele? Did you like her as a child?"

"Didn't we already discuss that?"

Knapp shot back a no-nonsense look.

"Well, I've always admired her and cared for her a great deal. She was
always a bit timid of me but, like Mother, I know she loved -- loves me."

"Quite right. She cares deeply about you."

"Yes, I know... I want to tell her, Knapp! I want to show her...! I
always did. 'But what if it scared her too badly?' I always thought. I could
never hurt her..."

"Of course not. But you didn't hurt *me,* remember."

"But she's never known about my other face, or even *asked!* I suppose
it never mattered to her. She's loved me regardless."

"What about women, Tristan? How do you feel about women in general?"

"Doctor Perrault once asked me about that. 'Do you like girls?' he asked.
"Do you?"

58

"I never met any, other than Anne, since I was very little. Mother used to take me outdoors for a walk...! I wanted to play with Anne's friends. They were mostly girls, I think."

"And now?"

"Oh, I would like to meet girls *very much!*"

"And why shouldn't you? Feel free to blush. It's quite natural."

Tristan stood and met Knapp eye-to-eye. "Come upstairs with me a minute."

They went upstairs.

A minute later, Tristan was showing him his collection of nude pictures taken from a dresser drawer.

Later, Knapp penned: "T apparently has no unhealthy sexual interests. In fact, he's shown me his art collection, some pages torn from books, which includes many female nudes. He's also admitted to some rather vivid erotic fantasies, all very normal for a lad his age (27). I've concluded that T's libido figures chiefly in his yearning to break free from his shell."

Not long thereafter, Anne Adele, now dressed for town, and Knapp were poised, ready to leave at the front door when Tristan appeared from behind them.

"Goodbye!"

She was startled at first. "Goodbye, Tristan."

"We'll be back soon," reassured Knapp. "Tristan, I'm just about to open this door... How would feel about seeing us off from the porch?"

He backed up two steps.

"I thought not."

Knapp pulled the door open wide as it would go. Tristan cowered but stood his ground. He saw Nicholas waiting by the family carriage out front.

"Don't let it trouble you," Knapp told his host. "I'm sure you'll feel ready... someday. Well, *au revoir.*"

Knapp exited with Anne Adele, closing the door behind them, then opened it again rapidly, making Tristan flinch again.

"Is there anything you'd like me to bring you?"

"I've arranged for Anne to do that, thank you." He managed a little smile.

Knapp nodded, smiled back and closed the door again. Tristan stood a moment longer, then backed away into the house.

Knapp maneuvered the team down one splendid avenue after another. Flights of wintering birds winged by above. Anne Adele kept mostly to herself at the start, but decided to speak her mind: "I know it's all for Tristan's benefit, and that sometimes you have to be cruel to be kind, but really, William, I hate to see you toy with him that way."

"I use tools, not toys... Anne, your strength has been a great help to me... You do approve of my intentions, if not my methods, I trust."

"I trust *you*, William... "

"Still, this 'affliction' of his occupies his mind every moment he's alive. He needs a jolt!" He tapped his temple. "Right here! A splash of cold water! He needs to forget – I wish I could tell you more."

They exchanged glances before he returned his concentration to the road.

She took the reins from him smoothly; he didn't resist. She slowed the carriage and guided it to a shady roadside orchard, small, dark apples spread everywhere.

She stopped the horses, dropped the reins and turned her face to his.

"What do you think you're doing?"

She took his hands in hers, leaned forward and kissed him.

"Anne Adele, I'm not sure this is wise."

"Just 'Anne', please... You feel just as I do. We're both strong... and beautiful. Let this be *our* secret, William."

They made love in the warm, shady breezes that caressed them both.

60

They might have heard a horse trotting closer and closer, then off, as Gilbert Thorndike rode past the orchard, oblivious to everything but his burgeoning thirst. He'd seen nothing he could use that day and was anxious for the comforts at Bégué's...

Nicholas had made a gumbo, seafood with rice for dinner. Knapp complimented his 'kitchen artistry' as Nicholas cleared the table settings.

Tristan coughed and said: "I must say I'm disappointed in both of you."

Knapp and Anne Adele paid instant heed.

"What do you mean?" she asked.

"You haven't said a word about your little jaunt through the neighborhood, either of you. How'd you like it, Knapp?"

"Like a grand tour. Splendid architecture... And there *is* a lazy, comfortable, atmosphere to the South. We practically had to *wade* through it. So -- hot and sticky! Come to think of it, it was rather *un*comfortable!"

The Duquesnes laughed.

"I'd expect that from a Yankee, suh!" affected Tristan as a plantation colonel, which tickled Knapp as well.

When the merriment subsided, Tristan and his stepsister shared a look; he took a paper-wrapped piece of chocolate from his pocket and presented it to Nicholas.

"Thank you, Master Tristan!" beamed the family servant gratefully, admiring and pocketing it before exiting with dishes.

"What was that all about?" inquired Knapp.

"It's an old custom of our kind, called a *lagniappe,*" Tristan explained.

"You see," Anne picked it up, "a master rewards his servant with a small gift to his liking for a job well done. And we know that Nicholas is partial to nut fudge, so Tristan asked me to get some when you and I went to the city."

Knapp's mind flashed back to his time with Anne in the city, so vibrant and gleeful in its anticipation of the holiday. And how she looked comparing dresses, trying on hats, as appealingly feminine as could be, as feminine as -- But Celia was worlds away.

"Mother gave them to all the servants when we had more of them living in," Tristan recalled. "Now there's only Nicholas, the first and the last of them… "

"I think it's a charming custom," agreed Knapp.

She smiled at him, which he saw, without acknowledgment.

"And the gumbo was delicious."

Hours later, in his robe, in his room, Knapp was reviewing and amending his journal when his door swung slowly open.

Anne entered, wearing only her chemise, and closed the door silently.

"Anne, no. Please!" he whispered. "This is wrong."

She embraced him. "You don't mean that."

He broke away. "Yes, I do."

"Wrong for whom? Tristan?"

"Yes, and for me too."

"You have a lover back in Boston," she intuited.

"My fiancée, yes. Poor Celia. I couldn't forgive myself if I -- "

"There's nothing to forgive. I don't want you for a husband, William… No one need ever know… "

She removed her undergarment. Knapp weakened at the sight of her ripe, beautiful body. They kissed. She removed his robe and turned down the lamp. They kissed once more and descended onto his bed…

Near dawn, Nicholas, only half-asleep, could hear the faintest sound of crying, but ignored it, as always.

Tristan paced nervously to and from the wall.

Anne Adele was seated on the downstairs parlor loveseat, attending the argument between Tristan and Knapp.

"And I tell you it's *too early* for such a step! I'm not ready for it!"

"Not ready even to *try?* This doesn't sound like you, Tristan."

"It's me, all right! And it's my opinion that the world is just as unready for *me!* Who's out there waiting for me, Knapp? More moonstruck libertines like Thorndike? What guarantees can you offer for my safety? "Civilization" hasn't been more corrupt since the days of the Roman Empire! New Orleans being particularly corrupt, what with this Storyville slum, all this gambling and prostitution -- and that wretched Mardi Gras...! Besides which, there are the epidemics, hurricanes, floods and Man himself racing about on wheels and in the air where he has no business whatsoever! It's a dangerous world full of dangerous excesses, Knapp, and I know I'd better be very careful before I -- expose myself to it."

Professor Knapp stood and swept the air with a dismissive palm. "Oh, enough of this bombastic excuse-making! Really! Have you been listening to yourself? I doubt very much whether you would be washed away by a flood or struck by a falling aeroplane if you just went outside for a bit of fresh air! Just a few steps past the door, out into the sunlight -- "

Tristan soured, sneering over his shoulder at him.

"My own words flung back at me, eh, Knapp? Is that how you do it? How you effect your cures? With guilty words? Well, I know my own mind. I won't be tricked by words."

Ignoring emotion, Knapp was steadfast. "May I remind you that your failure is our mutual failure? I can't help it if you yourself resist trying to make progress. Excuses are easier to make than progress, anyway."

"I won't be tricked, Knapp...! You'll say anything now to make your point."

"And you'll say anything to protect your cowardice."

Tristan seethed with wordless frustration.

"No one's trying to trick you into anything," said Anne Adele.

63

"Anne Adele, don't try to change my mind."

"I won't. But I will tell you that I'd be just as proud of you if you were only to face the open door at the threshold, for just a moment or two......"

Tristan looked at his feet. "And I'll admit – I'd *like* to do that, but – "

"Then you *should*,"Knapp prescribed.

Young Master Duquesne hesitated, then walked up to Knapp, who clapped him solidly on the shoulder and led him to the foyer, Anne Adele following. Tristan stopped short of it. Knapp rested his hand on the knob.

"Would you like me to open it?"

Tristan shook his head a bit and looked to Anne Adele.

Knapp humbly stood aside as she took his place.

Nicholas came in, looking quite concerned. "M'sieur!"

"Everything's fine, Nicholas," he was told. "I'll be right back."

Anne Adele held out her hand; Tristan took it. She opened the door. He began to heave with anxiety and shielded his eyes a few seconds, then held out his other hand; Knapp took it. She stepped out onto the porch.

Tristan made it as far as the door itself, then froze, quivering with anticipation and fear.

Knapp gently let go of his hand, and so did Anne.

Tristan quavered, alone on the threshold, another second or two before propelling himself forward by sheer force of will.

Knapp watched, barely keeping his elation in check as Tristan tottered out onto the porch, past Anne, down the steps to the pathway and into the sunlight.

Tristan turned to them and raised his arms a bit, his face a mixture of anguish and triumph.

He ran back toward Knapp and collapsed into his arms with great tears of joy. The teacher ushered him toward the steps. Anne Adele also wept with delight as they went back inside.

Nicholas, awed and abrim with happy pride, decided to keep the door open.

64

Unbeknownst to all, from a bushy covert nearby, Gilbert Thorndike lowered his binoculars in amazement as he stared at Maison Duquesne's open front door and declared: "He went for a little walk...!"

***

Chapter Nine

Omens

From the Duquesne carriage, Knapp got his second good look at New Orleans. Nicholas drove past an organ-grinder whose tethered monkey thrilled a gaggle of youngsters, and tradesmen decorating their storefronts. Customers streamed in and, either carrying or wearing an array of colorful outfits, out of a costumier's shop. People wearing or carrying huge, bizarre masks intermingled. Mardi Gras was coming!

Shortly, the two stopped in Congo Square for Nicholas's regular purchase from Crequeline Crozaix, whose followers eyed Knapp with disinterest or distrust.

66

"*Bonjour, Madame. Le charme blanc, merci,*" the Creole ordered, then to his companion said: "Crequeline Crozaix is the voodoo queen. You see, M'sieur le Professeur, although I am a Christian, I buy the voodoo charms, as did M'sieur Étienne for many years, for my Master's benefit. For the power they seem to wield."

"*Seem* 'to wield'?" Knapp half-smiled. "Are you *sure* you believe in them, Nicholas?"

Nicholas pointed to his purchase. "This one's for rest from worries. It has kept him sane all these years. Is that not proof?"

Knapp arched a brow. "Nicholas, my good fellow, I was keen to know what's in them, so Tristan told me — salt, saffron, gunpowder, and the principal ingredient is dried dog dung."

Whiskery chin thrust forward, Crequeline Crozaix corrected: "*Non, M'sieur!* The principal ingredient is *magic!*"

Knapp looked sharply at her. "I've heard that, yes."

Nicholas paid for the *gris-gris*. The witch-queen pulled her shawl tighter around her as they departed, as if a cold wind had chilled her bones — or perhaps her soul.

Upon returning to Maison Duquesne, Nicholas shut the stable door and and rejoined Knapp before going inside. The Professor handed him a paper-wrapped candy from his pocket.

"For a job well done," said Knapp with a half-bow. "It's a praline, I'm afraid. I couldn't find any nut fudge, but I thought you might like another flavor now and then."

"And so I do, Professor. You are very wise," smiled Nicholas, returning the nod.

Knapp smiled back and headed indoors.

The servant threw the candy to the ground without tasting it. "But I don't like pralines."

Coincidentally, Knapp was standing before the parlor window, admiring Nicholas's garden, when Anne strolled by outside with a watering can. He watched her moisten the flowers while he listened.

"Mardi Gras's nigh upon us, Knapp," Tristan muttered. "You shouldn't deny yourself the opportunity, really. I recommend it. From all I've heard and read about it. So, do go, with Anne Adele, naturally, and enjoy yourself..."

"I undoubtedly will...!" Knapp shrugged. He saw Anne coyly pretending obliviousness to his presence beyond the glass, and returned his to attention to her stepbrother.

"Tell me, Tristan, why do you dread this holiday so much...? An association with your father? Some unpleasant memory?"

"No... Because it seems a mockery to me... I always thought it was somehow a mockery *of* me... in theory, that is. The wearing of false faces, you know. I know that's just my interpretation of it, but I think it's... pagan as well. Unhealthy, dangerous. The crowds, the drinking, the profligacy, blood running hot. Father loved it, of course. He helped elect the King for several years... I can show you his collection of Mardi Gras photographs and Mother's illustrations, dating from eighteen-seventy-five to eighteen-eighty-four -- if you'd care to see...?"

Knapp turned from the window and bade Tristan lead the way.

A minute later, they were inspecting the contents of the Dusquesnes' Memory Book by the open drapes in the upstairs parlor.

"This may be the thousandth time I've looked at these," Tristan guessed. "There's Father."

He identified an 18th Century French lord standing amongst a gathering of revelers in eerie masks.

"He was almost elected Rex himself in eighteen-eighty-three, the year I was born -- "

His fingers pulled away the photo, revealing another, closer look at the senior Duquesne, affecting an appropriately haughty and cruel smirk.

68

"Then he resigned, withdrew completely -- which suited Mother just fine. She had no use for all that -- silliness."

Knapp extracted a drawing of a king throwing things from a gilded coach to a greedy throng. "And this would be Old Rex, eh? What's he throwing to them?"

"The enlightened rabble is scrambling for and squabbling over His Majesty's worthless beads and trinkets. It's never ceased to amaze and disgust me -- "

Knapp abruptly shut the Memory Book. "Are you ready for another stroll?"

He observed Tristan's expression transform from surly disapproval to placid self-awareness, with a delicate sigh and affirmative nod.

Leo Durant, the pudgy, spray-whiskered, familiar whitewing of Bourbon Street, swept the sidewalk outside Bégué's for the last time that week, fomenting eager thoughts of the celebration to come. He had his costume all ready to wear, and he licked his lips in anticipation of a long period of intoxication, his true passion in life.

Inside, the Bohemians enjoyed an early round of drinks, the first bottles empty by three o'clock.

"We are lazy good-for-nothings," claimed Karl, pulling a cork. "We should all be working, creating...!"

"Why are you so quiet today?" Madeleine asked Thorndike.

"Maybe he's getting inspired again, eh?" the overstuffed Korbecz winked.

"If I seem distant," deigned Thorndike, "it's because I have been very far from here... I have seen Tristan Duquesne! Face to face! *Twice* now!"

"Mother of God!" Madeliene crossed herself. "You didn't go *there*, did you?"

"I said I would, didn't I? Thorndike always keeps always keeps a pledge! And here is what I saw -- the face of Adonis! Not the Medusa!"

69

"No disease?" whimpered Karl. "Too bad."

"Yes, a genuine Adonis!" His eyes shone. "A countenance, a profile of such nobility and symmetry that only my chisel can do it justice! So now, more than ever, I must render him in clay! Or stone! But – I have a problem. I can't get his permission to sit for me!"

"I wish you'd leave the poor kid alone," Madeleine blinked at him. "You don't know what you're getting into."

"Did he remove his hood for you?" wondered Karl.

"Yes," lied Thorndike easily. "He humored me for a minute, but – his face was exposed for all to see! So why he wears a hood in the first place is a mystery to – even him!"

"I wouldn't ask questions if I were you," warned Madeleine.

"Maybe it's dandruff," burbled Korbecz, scratching beneath his beret, prompting some throaty chortles around the table.

"Don't joke about it!" shouted the Gypsy girl, crossing herself again.

"Wait! Here's an idea, Madeleine should dress for Mardi Gras as a nun!"

More laughter erupted.

"And you should go as a gentleman! No one would know you!" she shot back.

Thunderous, drunken laughter topped Thorndike's.

"Touché!" Thorndike surrendered. "Madame, another round!"

Some days later, the Sunday before the holiday, at dusk, Knapp and Tristan strolled the grounds near the willows. Knapp walked evenly, steadily, while the latter, talking animatedly, enlivened as he was by the new sensation of being outdoors, all but danced around his mentor.

"Exhilarating! The birds and the trees, Knapp! How well they live together! And how much more alive they seem outside!"

"Everything *is* more alive outdoors, my boy."

70

"I always envied Nature from my windows, you know. Yet I saw so little. The infinity of sky above us, only a patch heretofore! Insects, unseen! A breeze, unknown! Vast horizons all about me, and the very ground alive, pulsing, breathing with life only seen before, not felt...! It's a bit dizzying!"

Later, Knapp would journalize: "T is showing miraculous progress now, improving rapidly every day. Such are his good spirits and so strong his conviction to succeed, that he is now quite literally making strides outside his personal darkness."

From his covert, Gilbert Thorndike was unwilling to stop long enough to blot the sweat from his face as he toiled. He was crouched, alternately watching them through his field glasses and sketching swiftly, muttering criticisms and compliments at his work, until at length, he peered at the imminent sunset with a scowl.

"I'm losing the light...! That'll be enough for today, then," he groused to his distant subject.

Now Tristan was seeing a panorama of drifting clouds.

"This is a bit unnerving, really. But only if I stand still and stare at them," he told Knapp.

Nicholas came out onto the porch a second time, wearing an admonishing look. "Dinner-time, m'sieurs!"

"Don't chide *me*, Nicholas! Master Tristan is still exploring!"

"We're playing 'Lewis and Clark'!" Tristan laughed.

Nicholas suppressed a smile and retreated indoors.

"Oh, what a sunset!" Tristan marveled. "I could just touch it! I wonder if the stars --?"

His hood fell. The idiot Face began to awaken.

Knapp turned to ice. Aghast, the young man whirled on his heel and yanked the cowl back up again. They both looked around to see if anyone else had seen.

71

No one had. Thorndike was busy packing his sketchbook and binoculars into his saddlebag. In another few seconds, he was leaving his shady blind.

Tristan controlled his panic admirably. Still panting a little, he turned back to Knapp, speechless, ashamed that his self-confidence had been shaken so easily.

Knapp took him by the shoulder toward the house. "No harm done. Come on, let's have our supper."

They could hear a horse riding away, a common enough sound, so they thought nothing of it.

Following Nicholas's fine mutton stew and some hours' conversation in Tristan's parlor, mostly about Mardi Gras history, the Duquesnes and their guest reached a mutual accord to retire.

Anne Adele kissed Tristan's hands good night. Subdued, he returned the gesture silently. She smiled warmly, he sadly back at them before leaving.

She watched him close the parlor doors, then started downstairs.

In his bedroom, Tristan lifted the end of his mattress, said: *"Bon chance...!"* and dropped the end of the bed back into place. Unseen, two feathers flew out and wafted to the floor.

In the hallway leading to Knapp's room downstairs, he was just about to enter with his journal when Nicholas approached from the kitchen, wiping his hands with a towel.

"Anything else for you tonight, m'sieur?"

"Just this..." Knapp fished in his pocket, retrieved and handed him another sweet.

"Another *lagniappe!*" He opened it. "Praline!" he cooed. *"Merci, m'sieur.* Good night."

Knapp waited a moment; Nicholas popped it into his mouth with a grin.

"Good night."

72

Knapp went into his room and closed the door. Nicholas used the towel to remove the unwanted present from his mouth, shook his head glumly and returned to his kitchen.

Anne was already in William's room. Naked beneath her *peignoir,* she pulled him into an embrace as they kissed, and onto his bed. His journal fell to the carpet.

Outside, not far away, an owl hooted.

It is Mardi Gras at night! Knapp stands in the midst of a crowd of revelers wearing the variety of eerie masks he saw in Congo Square. As he walks amongst them, the masks loom larger and larger, pressing closer and closer until he can hardly move!

The masked Rex now arrives in his splendid coach. With stylized hauteur, he removes his bejeweled mask; Knapp sees it was Tristan! Flanked by Anne and Nicholas, he is dressed and bewigged as a French lord, they his lady and royal footman.

The giant masks all clamor for his gifts, a bobbing, barely controlled riot of clowns, beasts and knaves, noisily pleading and pressing with growing excitement. Knapp feels queasy; something is amiss.

Tristan Rex raises a hand. Holding a single chunk of nut fudge, he shows it archly all around, miming a fawning adoration of it, lastly to Knapp.

He begins to protest, desperately but pointlessly, as he is drowned out by the surrounding, roaring frenzy around him.

Tristan Rex teasingly dangles the bit of candy some more, then drops it with deliberate daintiness.

With a collective shriek, the masks twist around in unison, all baring the now-huge, now-crazed and furious face of Tristan's other side!

The king and his court laugh heartily, silently, holding their sides!

Knapp falls to his knees in horror as the monstrous icons engulf him! In his struggle to avoid being trampled, he grabs at the leg of a man wearing but one shoe. He looks up.

Étienne Duquesne glowers down at him. Slowly, he raises the other, gore-crusted shoe high overhead, and swings his weapon down at Knapp's head with mad ferocity --

Knapp sprang into a sitting position, hands held outstretched, then saw he was alone in the dark sleeping chamber. He rubbed his face hard, rubbed his neck, and hung his agonized head in relief before falling back, exhausted.

Then he heard the Voice, a weird, ululating cry, from upstairs. He sat up again, listening, fighting a chill the source of which was also born of nightmare.

***

Chapter Ten

An Accident

Monday was unanimously elected a day of complete rest. The only activities were performed by Tristan, who did his indoor walking exercises, and Anne Adele, who attended Mass by herself and prayed that his deliverance, whatever form it may take, be swift and clean, free of emotional strife for herself and all else concerned.

Knapp helped Nicholas in the kitchen a bit, preparing jambalaya.

At night, Nicholas played old favorites on the harmonium. Anne Adele talked about Baltimore, Knapp about Boston, his book's success and his meeting with Freud.

75

On Tuesday, the session was brief, as Tristan had trouble sleeping the night before, owing, he thought, to an overspiced meal for dinner, for which Knapp took culinary blame.

And this was not Tristan's favorite day, by any means. So he took to bed with the Professor's permission, and a dose of Nicholas's special remedy, just after one o'clock that afternoon.

Knapp joined Anne in the garden for an hour, assisting her make cuttings, before going back inside to accomplish the duty he'd promised himself to fulfill; he went to the parlor desk and wrote:

"My Dear Celia,
Good to hear from you. The weather here is fine, if humid, and the work's progressing excellently.

We are moving along so rapidly that I'll be back in Cambridge telling you about it before too long!

Must finish this quickly. Mardi Gras begins today, and my new friends and I have much to celebrate. I must help us prepare -
Yours,"

He signed and re-read it quickly, found an envelope, enclosed, sealed and stamped it, in time to hand it to Nicholas.

"If you will, here's a letter to be posted."

"Yes, m'sieur. Is there anything I can bring you from town?"

"Well, I could use some ink, as always."

"Very good, m'sieur. The same brand. Something else? Some pralines for yourself, perhaps?"

"No, nothing else, thanks."

Nicholas smiled. Knapp registered a delayed reaction, looking at him twice, then asked: "What are your plans for the evening, may I ask?"

"Knowing you've planned to stay here with Master Tristan," he answered, "Miss Anne Adele has asked me to accompany her to the city for an hour or two, or perhaps longer, to experience the festivities. It has been several years since her last."

"Well, enjoy yourselves. Stay out of trouble."

Nicholas's eyes widened. "Of course, m'sieur!" He exited with the letter.

Knapp lost himself in reverie. He considered what he'd written to Celia about helping to 'prepare' for Mardi Gras to be a lie, as he'd nothing to do but conduct another session with Tristan. – But a white lie, forgivable given the circumstances!

He'd go to the city with Anne later in the week, maybe tomorrow, and he'd 'prepare' for that, donning whatever mask and costume could be obtained for him, so it wasn't really a lie, ultimately...

He simply didn't know what to do about Anne other than to allow Nature to take her course – with all due precaution against complications, naturally.

But he couldn't tell Celia, ever.

Then it would be – a gentleman's secret. He felt his philosophy could live with that.

Eventually, Tristan came to the parlor, directly to Knapp, and shook hands.

"I just want to thank you, Knapp, for humoring me in staying with me today instead of indulging in – "

"You are more important to me than a party that will last long enough to see some of it, anyway... You're welcome. Now, the sofa, if you please."

Tristan took his position. "You will enjoy yourself, I daresay, Knapp."

"That's the whole idea, isn't it?"

"Unless you're me."

"Don't sulk... Think you'd like to take another walk today? Don't want to get fat on Fat Tuesday, do you?"

"You know I've come to enjoy one every day now."

"Then why not a *ride?*"

Tristan felt caught in a trap. "What, *now*, you mean?!"

"No, not yet. Nicholas has to go to the city. But when he returns, – "

Tristan knotted his fingers. "I don't think so, Knapp."

"A short tour of the neighborhood is all I'm suggesting. It'll be perfectly safe, I'm sure."

The fingers spread. "I don't feel it's time for that yet."

Knapp frowned. "You never do, do you? Yet it always works out, doesn't it?" He turned his back. "Very well, I won't force you, naturally. But... Anne Adele's promised to come along, in case you change your mind."

"You spoke to her this morning?"

"Why, er, yes. Every morning, usually..."

Now Tristan turned his back. "I don't know that I'm up to it... Not this day. It's too – unpredictable."

Anne entered the parlor and went to her stepbrother. She looked at him a moment, took his hands in hers, then gave him an unexpected hug.

Tristan recoiled slightly, more embarrassed than upset. He gazed outside and saw Nicholas drive the family carriage out at a slow clip. Anne and Knapp exchanged glances.

"Tristan," Knapp raised his voice a touch, "how can you know until you try?"

Tristan remained facing the window. "Very well, then. I'll go."

Anne started toward him, but a gesture from Knapp stopped her. She smiled at William. "Maybe a short walk first would help," she suggested.

Knapp smiled back.

Outdoors, the three ambled about beneath an overcast sky. It might even rain, Nicholas had guessed.

From his covert, Thorndike, ludicrously dressed up as Paul Revere, watched and persistently returned to his sketchbook to add details, while his mount grazed placidly. He wasn't very happy with the results, erasing and re-drawing impatiently. Another look through his spyglasses revealed something new --

The Creole butler was guiding the Duquesne carriage to the roadside, the others joining him, including Tristan.

"He's leaving! He's leaving the grounds!" he keened.

The sister was helped inside the coach by Knapp. Then he helped the young master of the house board as well before getting in himself.

"He should be congratulated, the brave soul...! And why not?!"

Gilbert Thorndike pulled his horse away from its clover luncheon, packed his saddlebag and reset his tri-cornered hat.

They all sat facing forward, Anne between the two men.

Nicholas sat atop the vehicle, reins at the ready, awaiting word.

Tristan was still jittery, looking back toward the house.

"Are you comfortable, Tristan?" asked Anne Adele.

"I'm sure I will be soon... We won't go far, you say?"

"No," said Knapp. "Are you sure you *want* to go?"

He smiled at Knapp. "I suppose it's time... Anne, take my hand."

She did.

"Are you ready?"

Tristan nodded once, tautly.

"All right, Nicholas!"

The reins gently snapped, the horses began at a slow trot.

Tristan was riveted to his seat with childlike fear.

Knapp observed. "How are we doing so far?"

"I -- I'm not -- The sensation of motion without effort is -- unsettling," reported the first-time passenger anywhere.

79

"You'll get used to it in no time," Anne predicted.

"I'd better... or I'll regurgitate."

Knapp feigned shock. Anne laughed. Tristan gave them an uneasy look.

The team continued steadily, passing the first house as the sun broke out from behind the clouds.

"You were wrong, Nicholas!" shouted Knapp.

"M'sieur?"

"No rain!"

"Non, m'sieur! Clear skies after all!"

"There is no end of jostling to this, I see," Tristan complained, adjusting himself and avoiding the outside view.

"You're not seeing the sights," Knapp noted aloud.

"Do look out the window, Tristan," Anne Adele agreed, "You always do at home now."

He did, and saw with interest the surroundings speed by!

He felt better about the minor physical discomforts and mentioned it to them, along with his impressions of passing birds in flight, of people and things coming and going from his perspective, an exciting introduction to travel, all new and not at all as frightening as he'd first imagined.

"Feeling better now, eh?"

"Look at that house! It's gorgeous!" He shielded his eyes. "And the sun's out now! Oh, Knapp, I'm glad you talked me into this! I've never had such an experience!"

"We knew you'd be thrilled." Anne swelled with gladness and relief.

"Now the only problem is adjusting my eyes!"

Behind the carriage, Thorndike rode in, steadily drawing closer.

"You don't mind the motion itself now?" Knapp inquired.

"Mind it? It's invigorating! But I do wish Nicholas would slow down around corners!"

"I'm going as slowly as possible, Master Tristan!"

80

Crossroads loomed ahead.

"Let's take this road!" Knapp shouted to Nicholas, "To the left!" and asked Tristan: "Are you all right? Like to turn back?"

As he neared the turn to the left, Nicholas saw that a rider starting to pass on his left, not only easily but rapidly.

Despite the costume, the servant recognized him. "*You!*"

Thorndike grinned at him, then looked ahead and realized he was being squeezed between the carriage and the turn. So he yanked on his reins with a yell, halting his steed abruptly in front of the Duquesne carriage. His horse reared up.

Nicholas likewise tugged the team's reins violently to one side. Thorndike tried to swing around, out of the carriage's way as the team swerved dangerously, whinnying fearfully, eyes wide, and hooves flailing.

Tristan, Anne and Knapp froze in shock.

The two-horse team tumbled sideways to the ground, twisting the coach over onto its side, topside wheels spinning.

Thorndike managed to control his mount, watching the accident he caused unfold with guilty remorse.

Anne and Tristan, still holding hands, were thrown from the carriage. His forehead hit the top jamb of the flung-open door, knocking him out, hood flying back. As they landed, sprawling onto the ground, their hands released each other. She was shaken but still conscious, he on his back.

Knapp, still inside the overturned coach, moaned and began to extricate himself as Nicholas, yards away, winded, stood and clutched at his ribcage. The team, writhing on their sides, scrambled back upright, uninjured.

Anne crawled to her stepbrother's side.

The eyes of the Face fluttered open, no longer blind. They seemed to recognize a predicament in progress, and the next face in view.

Anne reached Tristan's side, saw the Face that had been hidden by the hood all her life, screamed and fainted dead away.

81

Knapp, electrified, pulled himself out in a hurry, discovering his left arm was sprained, and strained to reach the Duquesnes. He could see that Tristan's secret had been exposed.

Thorndike spurred his horse to draw nearer. Riding closer, he gasped as he too saw the Face; his steed stopped short and shied. The upstart sculptor stared down at the sight incredulously as his horse bucked and snorted.

From a kneeling position, Knapp pulled the fallen hood back in place with his right hand and glared up at Thorndike.

"Damn you, you maniac!" he roared, then set about tending to Tristan and Anne.

Nicholas, as steadily as possible, grabbed the loose reins of the team and tied them to a nearby tree, then, shaking his fist at the careless horseman, hurried to the aid of the others.

"*Nom du chien!* You crazy dog! When I get my hands on you, I'll twist your stupid neck! As I should have done the first time I saw you!" Nicholas advanced on Thorndike, whose lips were curled in repulsion.

"Oh, no... *Oh, no!*" was all he could manage to say.

Nicholas reached for his reins. But the sculptor came to his senses fast enough to snap them away and make his escape, still shrieking: "*No, no, no, no!*"

Muttering curses, the servant exhaled painfully and returned to Knapp's side.

"He's been knocked unconscious. Could be a concussion. Still, we have to move him," the Professor ordered.

"To the hospital?"

"I'm not sure yet. See to Anne, will you? She may have broken something."

"M'sieur! Your arm!"

"Yes, it's sprained, at least. What about you?"

"A broken rib or two, I think."

"We'll call a doctor from the house."

82

They uprighted the carriage and put the Duquesnes back inside. Knapp untied the reins and handed them off, boarded carefully, and Nicholas headed the team back down the road to Maison Duquesne.

***

Chapter Eleven

The Awakening

Shortly thereafter, Tristan lay upon the sofa, still unconscious. Anne Adele, who had come to during the short ride back and could only stare silently at Tristan, sat, now feeling her neck gingerly. Nicholas was on the telephone, Knapp waiting close by.

"Yes, madame. Thank you, madame." He hung up and told Knapp: "Doctor Patterson is leaving now. He should be here very soon."

"Hopefully, it's not too serious. It doesn't seem to be any worse than a bad bump."

"I'll see what I can find in the medicine cabinet that might help."

84

"Yes, thank you..."

As Nicholas left, Knapp looked at Tristan, still supine, and shook his head in defeat.

"William, I *saw* it." Anne was at his elbow.

"I thought as much... Anne, I'm sorry."

"Don't you feel badly. You couldn't have known this would happen."

"I mean I'm sorry you learned about it this way. *He* wanted to tell you -- would have in time..." Knapp was lost in himself. "What should I say when he awakens?"

"Maybe I should tell him," she thought.

"Perhaps that'd be best..." he mused, then, frustrated, reconsidered: "No, I must tell him!" He sat, head in hands. "Oh, Lord, I've violated his trust."

"No, you haven't," Anne corrected, "I should have known long ago. There must have been a hundred things I can think of now that should have told me before this... How I pity him, William... They looked at me, those strange eyes. They knew who I was."

"It must have seemed that way to you, Anne, but -- it's impossible. Those eyes are blind."

By late afternoon, Mardi Gras festivities had commenced. The streets of the French Quarter were filled with masked and costumed revelers drinking and carousing openly.

Thorndike emerged from a public livery, still jittery from his experience. He pushed his way through the crowd across the street and entered his old apartment building. He hurried up the rickety stairs to his second-story loft, found his key with twitching fingers and let himself in, breathlessly collapsing against the door once inside.

Outside, an oncoming parade marched into earshot.

He secured the heavy beam in place to barricade himself, and tested it for good measure.

85

He looked about nervously, but only saw his easel and drying canvas, his old sculptures and tools, his cot, empty gin bottles, cobwebs, his grimy window, and nothing else.

One thought occurred to him: to find a full bottle of anything. He did, and took two, long, straight gulps. He huddled himself in the wide, dust-layered windowsill.

The parade carried on below, but he didn't really notice, his distant gaze still ashine with horror. His vigil of terror had begun. Without knowing how, yet he sensed the worst was coming...

Elderly, goateed Dr. Patterson finished examining Tristan's injury while the others stood in anxious attendance. Knapp now wore a sling for his left arm.

"It's probably not a concussion, but it's not far from it. I wish you hadn't moved the body. You might've hurt him worse."

"I – thought he was just unconscious."

"We all did," Anne Adele said. "But then, when he wouldn't wake up – "

"That's as may be," Dr. Patterson chided, "but it still doesn't explain to me why you won't let me remove this thing from his head so I can examine him properly."

"We looked," covered Knapp. "There was nothing there."

"Well, I'll take your word for it, Doctor –?"

"Doctor Knapp. From Boston." He didn't feel his correct title mattered just then.

"Oh, really...?" the older gentleman replied. "Well, I still say the best place for him is – "

"We appreciate your coming, Doctor Patterson, especially tonight, but I'll take care of the rest, if you please," interrupted Knapp, handing him his hat and coat.

"But wouldn't you like me to bandage –?"

86

"I'll take care of it, Doctor. I just thought I'd better make sure. Obtain a second opinion, so to speak."

"And I've done my share of nursing duties for children's charities in Baltimore," Anne added.

Nicholas fetched Patterson's black bag and gave it to him, then helped see him to the door.

"So thank you," smiled Knapp.

"Whatever you say, *'Doctor'...!* There's just one more thing. I charge two dollars for an emergency house call. And I'd appreciate payment for my trouble *now!*" He thrust his palm forward.

Knapp paid him. "Thank you again, and good night."

"I can't remember the last time such rude treatment has come my way! No manners! I swan! No wonder you' all hermits!"

Nicholas closed the door after him.

"Why did I lie to him?" pondered Knapp aloud. "I'm beginning to distrust my own motives."

Nicholas raised a finger. "It's not wise, Professor, to share a secret with everybody."

A thought struck Knapp. "Nicholas, did *you* see beneath the hood?"

"I did not, m'sieur. Nor would I need to. I know what must be there — evil."

Tristan stirred.

"It's *not* evil! — He's coming to." To Anne, he whispered: "Be careful what you say..."

Tristan sat straight up, then turned to Anne, saying coldly: "So... You've finally seen it."

"How did you know that?!" Knapp marveled.

"This is just how I've always expected you to look... your face filled with helpless, hateful pity. No more of that, thanks!"

"You need rest, Tristan," suggested Anne.

"There's nothing to worry about," Knapp supposed.

"Who else saw it...?   Nicholas?"

Nicholas, intently concerned, didn't move a muscle.

"No, he's been loyal," he knew.

Then, coiling with hatred: "It was the artist Thorndike who was there, wasn't it?"

"Yes," averred Knapp, *He* caused the accident, and *saw*...   Apparently the man cannot help being a fool."

"He hasn't been the *only* fool, *has* he, Knapp?"

"Tristan!" exclaimed Anne.

"I told you we were going too fast!   Now my disgrace will become a public matter!"

"Nicholas, please," instructed Knapp, "some warm milk for your master."

"Oh, stop playing "Doctor", Knapp!"

Knapp spoke to Nicholas again: "As Miss Anne Adele says, he needs his rest." The butler nodded and exited to the kitchen.

"As you and Anne need yours, eh?" snarled Tristan.

Knapp gave him a suspicious look as she knelt by Tristan's side.

"You'll be all right," she told her stepbrother.   "Everything will be all right.   We had a doctor in for you -- Doctor Patterson -- Perrault's old friend!"

"Did *he* see too?!"

"He did not see," said Knapp.   "I wouldn't let him."

"Small comfort, 'Doctor'!   Soon the whole world will be talking about "The Freak of Carrollton"!   Better start writing your next book now, so you can --!"

*"Stop that this instant!"*Knapp demanded.

"This is *your* fault, Knapp...!   *Your* fault!"   Tristan was adamant.

Eyes welling up, Anne took Tristan's hand; he pushed it away savagely. She wept softly.

Knapp, shaken, admitted: "Of course, you're right. It is. I am to blame. I hope in time you'll forgive me. You made it my job to try and help you..."

"'In time'. eh? Well, now I've run out of time, thanks to you... Too fast, knapp. You went too far, too fast..." He passed out from the strain.

Nicholas returned from the kitchen. "The milk has turned, m'sieur; it has spoiled... Is he – asleep?"

"Yes. It can wait for now," Knapp told him. "I daresay we all need rest after such an ordeal. If it is indeed over."

"Don't take his words to heart, Professor. It's just one of his moods. It'll pass."

"Yes, he's thrown tantrums before, William."

"You're both very kind... I think the best thing for us to do now is to take him – all of us – to the hospital."

"Must we?" begged Anne.

"Professional, private care is better than a yard full of Thorndike's goggling friends, yes."

"But Tristan would object!" she protested. "Not only to being taken from here, but to a *hospital* –! He dreads them! Both his parents died in one!"

"And both of yours. I know... Well, as long as none of us are seriously hurt, I suppose we could wait till morning to make our decision. Meantime, let's all get some sleep. In fact, I'll stay here in case he should wake up."

"It's really *his* decision though, isn't it?" she asked.

"We'll see how we all feel in the morning," was all Knapp could think of to say.

Anne smiled compassionately at Knapp, then at Tristan. She knelt by him again and raised his hand gently, at first to kiss it, but changed her mind and rested it at his side instead, before retiring.

Nicholas's deep voice proposed: "He should be asleep in his own bed for the *gris-gris* to work properly."

"Best not to move him now," Knapp precluded.

Nicholas nodded as Knapp picked up his pen and sat at his journal on the desk.

"There is a new bottle of ink for you, m'sieur."

"Thank you, Nicholas. In the morning, we'll discuss what to do next – with fresh minds."

"Yes, m'sieur... Get some rest yourself, hear?"

"Soon, my good man, soon..."

Nicholas pressed at his sore ribs and exited, favoring them. Knapp dipped his pen and began writing:

"What has happened today represents both the zenith and nadir of our work here so far. I took the carriage ride, but that imbecile Thorndike managed to interfere again, and has caused a damnable accident."

Tristan, still asleep, turned his face into the sofa. In so doing, his hood slipped back halfway.

Knapp then heard a reedy, crackling Voice pierce the stillness of the parlor. It had a bit of motor difficulty at first, but corrected itself, next speaking quite fluently, in a tone containing rational intellect: "Wil-liam... E-ras-mus – Knapp!"

The Professor's eyes darted to Tristan. He involuntarily braced himself against his chair, then rose and crossed, as if hypnotized, to the sofa. He cautiously pulled the hood down the rest of the way, revealing the Face. Its eyes were looking straight at him with full understanding, and even benevolence.

Knapp was stunned, terrified, but listened, enraptured. Unmindful of it, he fell into a gradual crouch.

"I know – that I must seem to you a thing out of nightmares, but hear me, I beg you," pleaded the Voice.

90

The psychologist strove as never before to control his reactions to what followed:

"Please utilize your great, understanding nature in hearing my words, not your fear... How I have come to speak to you at this time is but one of the many mysteries of the human mind. And y
ou must know that I am part of Tristan and have always been so. Yet I am separate... I use his stored memory and a fuller portion of our shared brain due to the carriage accident. But that was mere circumstance. I have always been here, lying dormant, waiting for life, if ever, to come. Now I am here, and time is short. You must listen..."

Knapp, overcome by the miraculous sight and sound of this wise and superior new entity, began to weep. All else he could do was watch and listen, spellbound.

"Do not fear these mysteries, William. You must continue your studies of the inner mind, although its secrets may be both wondrous and tragic. Sometimes, tragedies help... Fear me not, William Knapp...! Darkness will eventually find the light that caused its shadow to be. They always meet, shadow and light... Learn from this tragedy, William. Show light to darkness, and all fears, all woes, all evil shall in time be banished..."

The Face smiled sorrowfully at Knapp, whom the encounter had left speechless. The eyes closed suddenly, tightly. The mouth moved as if choking.

Tristan awoke. He sat up and held his head in pain.

A thought struck Knapp, one so horrible, he could hardly speak: "No... No! Don't wake up *now!*"

Even as he said it, he felt a fool, for it had been inevitable. He stood, then sat to ground himself.

"Did you say something, Knapp?" mumbled Tristan, before coming fully to with a chill --

"Who else has been here?!"

He felt his hair and scalp – naked. "My hood!"

He stood straight up and walked to a wall mirror, simply staring at himself. Then he turned swiftly –

The Face, still exposed, saw itself for the first time, and regarded itself with deepest despair; the Voice groaned, low and forlorn.

His fingers clawing upward, Tristan uttered a single, soul-spearing shriek.

Knapp was galvanized, stuck to his seat.

"I can see –!" bellowed Tristan, stomping away from the mirror. "Through *his* eyes...! *Both* sides of the parlor at once!"

He gripped an arm of the sofa in terror, then leapt to his feet, enraged, as the Face shut its eyes.

"I *knew* it! I *knew* this was coming! I *always* knew *this* was coming! Your 'Frater Dementis', Knapp! He's come to *take me over,* come to stake his claim to *his* half of this body – *My* body! *My* life!"

Knapp staggered to his feet and approached him, his knees weak. "Tristan, you don't yet understand – "

"Hypocrite!"

The Face rejoined them. "Tristan...?"

The maddened Tristan paid sudden attention to this next entirely new sensation, jerking his shoulders as if to see whoever was behind him.

"You must calm yourself before it is too late. You must either accept me, now and always, or – "

Tristan uttered a fearful yelp, then felt at his throat's vibrations with slowly-dawning repugnance, as the Voice went on:

" – or we shall perish together this very night! Try to comprehend there is no reason for alarm. Although you can see through new eyes as well as your own, and hear a new voice from within, we are still one and the same. Two inhabiting one. You see through my eyes, and I through yours... Our thoughts will remain separate. You will remain separate. You will remain Tristan

Beaumarchais Duquesne. Only, you must allow me my existence, for we share the same brain, and so -- "

Tristan returned to the mirror.

"– *if you go mad, so must I –!*"

"No!" he shouted to his reflection in wild frustration. "Why do you come *now?!* Why do you *torment* me?! This is my body, do you hear? *My* body that houses the curse! *My brain* that feeds you, parasite! *My* soul you've eaten away! You've come to drive me insane, haven't you?! To *finish* the job?!"

He tore at his hair and swiveled viciously to face Knapp.

Knapp found voice enough to prevent further tirade.

"Tristan, I entreat you! Stop and think! Listen to your brother! He is not mad! He spoke to me! He has angelic intelligence! *Listen to me – to him! There is no such thing as 'Frater Dementis'!* It is *you* who are the dangerous one now, Tristan...!"

"I won't hear you, Knapp!" He turned his back and pointed with both hands to his other Face. "See where your good advice and logical questions and exercises have led me?! *Into Hell!*"

"I never meant – "

"I won't hear you, Knapp! And I swear I won't have a parasite! In fact, I'll end this right now!"

He lunged toward the desk as he ranted on, pulling out more hair. "After all, Knapp, – After all, 'Am I my brother's keeper?!'" he laughed. "The Bible also says: – "He struck the Face with rage-red fists. "Get thee *behind* me, Satan!' – And so he has!"

He found a paperweight on the desk and took aim with it at the back of his head, but Knapp hooked Tristan's arm with his good one. Infuriated, the younger man flung him to the open wall with a loud thud.
Nicholas arrived hurriedly in his nightshirt, but stood rooted to the spot when he saw his master's secret finally exposed.

93

"Keep back, I warn you, Nicholas!" Tristan grimaced.

"Tristan, please —!" pleaded the Voice.

Tristan swung an accusing finger toward Knapp. "*You're* to blame for all this! *You* made this happen — *on purpose!* *You* should be made to suffer as *I* am suffering — *as you made me!*"

"Please! Listen to reason! *Use* your reason!" begged the Voice.

"Out of the mouths of babes', eh?" Tristan slapped the Face viciously. "Be still! Children should be *not* seen and *not heard!*"

As he attempted to pull up the hood, Knapp rushed him again, grabbing one of his arms. "Tristan, don't —!"

Nicholas's hesitation ceased; he took his master's other arm. But Tristan's newfound strength pushed them both off with ease. Emboldened, he attacked Knapp again, trying to strangle him. He pulled the telephone's cord from the wall and wrapped it around his neck, pulling hard, pushing the chin back.

"Nicholas! Stop him! You must stop him!" cried the Voice.

Nicholas sprang into action anew, pinning one of Tristan's arms behind him and slamming him into a wall. Both halves of him unconscious again, he slumped to the floor.

"Thank you..." gasped Knapp. "This monstrous turn of events — not his fault..."

"Sit down and rest," said Nicholas. "I'll take care of this." He then began to tie Tristan's wrists with the telephone cord as Knapp wobbled upright as best he could.

"No time to sit. I'll be fine... We must take him to a hospital now. No, we'd have to tie him to the seat. Better call for an ambulance... "

Nicholas displayed the loose end of the cord.

"Oh, I see. We'll use a neighbor's telephone."

"Yes, m'sieur."

"I'm sorry you had to *see* this way, Nicholas."

"Let us say I was meant to see... that Fate would have it so." He stood, remembering: "Do you know... this is just the way I had to subdue M'sieur Étienne three years ago?!"

"Yes, and his son has chosen to relive that tragedy..." He looked up at Nicholas. "Do you know what he said to me, his other Face? 'Show light to darkness, and –"

" – all fears, all woes, all evil shall in time be banished.' I have spoken these words to Master Tristan many times before, having heard them from my own mother back in Saint Dominique long ago..."

"I still feel at fault."

"No, that is nonsense." scowled the old Creole. "All of us should have known better. And yet, some things grow out of hand all by themselves..."

He pulled Tristan up onto his side as Anne entered.

"What's happened here?!"

Knapp went to her and held her hands.

"Tristan's grown violent. But don't be alarmed. He's safe now. We're calling an ambulance."

She tightened her grip on his.

"We *must*, Anne Adele!" His intensity impressed her. "Public or not, a hospital's the only place for him now. He's undergone an almost complete personality change. Indeed, there's another – !" He stopped himself, then reconsidered: "But perhaps this madness is only temporary, until he gets – used to things."

She and Nicholas saw each other's eyes.

"You've seen too," she said flatly.

"Yes, Miss Anne Adele."

Knapp seized her firmly by the forearms. "You were right, Anne. You did see intelligence in those eyes. There never were eyes less blind. You should have heard what he told me. In fact, I must write down – "He

95

searched for and found his journal on the floor. " -- as much as I can remember."

Nicholas urged: "The ambulance, m'sieur?"

"Yes, bring the carriage 'round."

"My own mount would be faster."

"No, Anne's going with you."

"Going where?" she asked as Nicholas made for the kitchen. "But he's my --!"

"Please, don't object," he purred. "To stay may mean dire consequences."

Nicholas hitched the team to the buckboard just outside the stable, hearing the worlds-distant music of Mardi Gras. Espying the full moon above, he quickened his pace.

In Congo Square, Mardi Gras gave wide berth to the voodoo sect as Crequeline Crozaix presided over a somber ceremony. She grasped a snake in each brown, spotted, waxen hand. One of them bit her; she dropped the reptile, which slithered off. The ritual stopped in deadly silence. Followers treated and dressed her left hand as she gazed up at the bright, full moon and furrowed her brow.

"Soon," was all she said.

Thorndike changed clothes, no longer planning to enjoy the holiday with his friends.

He threw back the last of that last bottle, and remained looking at the golden moon above the noisy city as he let the empty vessel drop to the loft floor.

He forced himself to look away, at anything, at the Dixieland band passing below the window where he still sat, trying not to think, or remember...

***

Chapter Twelve

The Rise of Frater Dementis

Nicholas was just bringing the Duquesne carriage to the front of the house. He hurried up the steps.

Knapp escorted Anne from the parlor to the foyer and opened the door.

"Yes, of course I'll ride with him," Knapp told her. "We'll see you at Charity Hospital shortly."

"I hope you'll both be safe," she said, and kissed him.

Nicholas came to the door, the first to see what was just emerging from the parlor. Knapp and Anne turned. The men stared in awe; she held back a scream.

Tristan was standing just inside the foyer, clutching the sides of his head, quaking with madness, eyes glazed. The telephone cord dangled in shreds from his lacerated wrists.

Outside, an owl sounded its call and the horses snorted and stamped in fear.

"They've *seen*...! They've *all* seen!" Tristan said to himself.

"Tristan, no, *please!*" the Face, the Voice entreated.

Anne and Knapp embraced, both shivering with terror. Nicholas could only gape.

"Hush!" Tristan hissed sardonically, with an admonishing finger upheld to his brother's view. "You've got to be *brave!* And *continue* to be brave!"

"Tristan, I can save us!"

"And all fears, – "

"Give me control!"

" – all woes, – "

"Give me control! I must take control!"

" – all evil shall in time – be banished!"

"Tristan, please! *I beg you to listen to me!*"

"Get away from me!"

Tristan swerved around, crashing into Anne and Knapp, who flew apart from each others' arms. He lurched ahead, now before Nicholas the open door. The tortured, shaking figure battled on with itself, catching himself on the door jamb, and splintering it with his grip to the astonishment of all.

"They've all *seen!* I must *kill* them – *all!*" ranted Tristan.

The horses struggled to break free of their harness.

Dark birds winged past the clear ochre moon.

Nicholas, stiff with shock, saw the superhuman lunatic let go of the wooden frame and claw the air with bloodied fingers as if about to strangle the servant.

But then, he stopped himself, or so it seemed.

"No!" the other side shrieked.

Next moment, Knapp and Anne stepped aside automatically as Tristan careened backward, striking the wall with terrific force, but not enough to knock him out. He stumbled forward, every limb trembling, to the center of the foyer.

"No-o-o-o-o--!" the voices cried in unison, and Tristan collapsed onto the floor, dead to all appearances.

Anne whimpered helplessly. Knapp tried to comfort her as Nicholas stepped in closer for a better look at his fallen master.

But before anyone could find words to speak, the body on the floor began to stir with an uncanny, new sense of motion. The three onlookers froze anew.

Where Tristan last stood now arose, in awkward, almost involuntary, but powerful spasms, an entirely new being, but one being at last.

It tottered in place for a few seconds, breathing heavily.

The look on what had been Tristan's face now showed it to be a being that is evil incarnate...

It grinned at Anne, Knapp and Nicholas daringly. He could see they were all scared witless.

The terrible entity took one step, then appeared to have a stroke. The mad face of Tristan went slack and became one of an idiot.

Then, haltingly, but with determination, the thing turned in place.

With a low growl, the expression of its ugly other side had changed to one of pure malevolence. And it was now in control.

Frater Dementis, the mad brother, had come to life.

Knapp and the others couldn't believe their eyes as next, like a baby just learning to talk, it attempted its first, choking word, repeating the last word it had heard. Its voice is an unearthly pairing of the two brothers', a cold, wailing whisper with a liquid echo.

"No... no... no... No!" it smiled gleefully, a proud toddler.

It then assumed a predatory mien, stalking its prey, stiff-legged, -- backward, -- arms reaching out -- behind it.

99

Knapp shielded Anne; they backed up to the staircase. Nicholas's eyes stayed fixed on that infant creature of evil.

Frater Dementis spun suddenly to face the door again, showing Tristan's face to Anne, who was moved instantly to tears. With a maniacal twist, the demon swiveled in place to face Anne and Knapp again, but without moving its feet --

Its legs twining, its ankles snapped with a sickening crackle.

Snarling at them with its small, dreadful face, it untangled its lower limbs with improved mobility, though its feet now pointed behind it. It shambled slowly backward toward them, its knees popping as they dislocated to bend the other way.

It raised its arms very purposefully, backward. Again, bones broke and reset themselves preternaturally as it continued to stalk them. Its grasping hands also twisted and snapped into new position, upside-down.

Knapp tripped on the bottom step, bringing Anne down with him.

It was then that Nicholas jolted into action, attacking Frater Dementis in a rush. The former face of Tristan blindly snapped its teeth as it reached backward, more bones cracking, to threaten the servant.

But it only placed its inverted hands on his shoulders and brushed him off like a leaf. Next, the horrid face now burst into crocodile tears, along with the former Tristan, wheedling: "Oh, why are you afraid, Tristan? *There is no such thing as -- Frater Dementis!*".

With a demoniacal laugh in their faces, the fiend dashed awkwardly but steadily upstairs past Anne and Knapp, now standing again at the bottom.

Halfway up, still laughing in its calliope-like voice, it turned and confronted them imperiously.

"What do you want of us?" Knapp ventured bravely.

Its answer was brightly cheerful: "I'd like to hold your guts in my hands, if you don't mind, and squeeze them into rotting pulp! But first, a little game of Jekyll and Hyde -- and Seek! -- Literary humor, Knapp!"

100

Wracked with wild laughter once more, Frater Dementis ran up the rest of the steps and turned a corner, out of sight to those below. Breathless, shaken, the three converged at the foot of the stairs.

"Come and find me, Doctor Knapp! And cure me, please!" came the snidely playful call from above.

"What's happened here?! I don't understand!" Anne cried.

"No time to analyze now. That horrible creature is no longer Tristan," Knapp stated as calmly as he could.

"We must not go up there," Nicholas intercepted. "Two have become an unholy one. And he means to murder us. Evil has defeated our best intentions."

"Not yet!" Knapp found new resolve. "We must bring it down -- *kill* it if necessary, before it kills *us...!*" He turned, eye-to-eye with Anne. "Do you agree?"

She wrung her hands. "Yes, I agree... If only to end his suffering."

"Then we'd better arm ourselves." Knapp moved to the parlor, where Nicholas fetched two fireplace pokers, handing one to Knapp. "M'sieur, -- these should do."

Anne recalled: "I know where Father kept a pistol --!"

"Let's have it."

She found it in a table drawer and brought it to Nicholas, taking his poker in trade. "You've handled firearms before, I know."

"Let us pray it does not come to that, Miss Anne Adele."

Then, another cry from above, plaintive and pathetic: "Knapp! Anne! Save me! Nicholas, please! Come and save m--!" The voice sounded suddenly, forcibly muffled.

Anne bolted, but Knapp stopped her.

"No, Anne. Don't be fooled. If that -- being is as remotely intelligent as I believe it is, it is doubtless trying to lure us into some diabolical trap. There's no telling what this evil genius may have in mind!"

101

"I may be able to reach him, William."

"I doubt it. That thing wants us dead. But if we leave now, it may seek out others to attack and destroy. We must strike *now!*"

He looked from her to Nicholas, who nodded sharply, affirmatively, once.

"Anne, you wait in the carriage."

"No, William. If there's just a chance that I can help him, I will. I've got to try. And I won't let you leave me alone," she entreated, convincingly.

Knapp studied her resolute expression with annoyance, and then concurred with a heavy sigh: "Up we go, then."

The three took stock of themselves, their weapons, and each other before mounting the stairs.

They made hardly a sound as they finished their ascent.

They saw the parlor doors wide open, the room empty.

They proceeded down the hallway, stopping outside the master bedroom doors, which were open just a little.

"Tristan...?" Anne softly called.

Knapp hushed her; she bit her lip.

Nicholas stepped ahead of them and bade them silently to step back; they complied. He raised his pistol and used it to nudge the door open wider. Then he entered the bedroom, finger tight on the trigger.

At the foot of the bed, "Tristan" knelt, weeping soundlessly, exaggeratedly, his fingers locked in prayer before him. Then "he" spoke, in Tristan's old voice: "Nicholas! I've learned my lesson, old friend! 'Show light to darkness!'"

Nicholas took aim, but hesitated, moved by this bathos.

Knapp and Anne watched from the hall through the doorway as the sly thing, still facing Nicholas as Tristan, began to cry aloud, a child's cry, twisting its broken arms out to embrace the confused servant, who backed up out of their sight behind the door.

"Shoot him! *Kill him!*"Knapp shouted, taking Anne brusquely into his arms.

But now Frater Dementis leapt to its feet in a flash and swatted away the pistol. It grabbed thunderstruck Nicholas by the nape and mock-politely produced the *gris-gris* ball from its pocket with its other adverse hand.

"Your *lagniappe,* m'sieur! For a job well done in this life! And I hope it is to your liking!"

It shoved the feathery sphere squarely and fiercely into Nicholas's mouth. He gagged on the voodoo charm, and while he struggled to remove it, Frater Dementis swung around the elder Creole, pinned his arm behind him and pushed him face-first into the wall, with such force that he was embedded there.

The mad little face beamed with satisfaction.

Knapp and Anne couldn't see what had happened from where they stood.

"Nicholas!" cried Anne.

She and Knapp watched in bewildered dread as piece by piece, the pistol was thrown out the bedroom door to their feet.

"You won't use *this,* Knapp, and *neither will I!*"promised the monster.

Knapp took Anne by the shoulders, emphasizing his words with physicality. "Listen to me -- Go downstairs. Get into the carriage. And be ready to take it yourself if I don't come back out. I intend to kill that ungodly thing."

He propelled her toward the stairs and raised the poker high as he entered the bedroom.

About to descend, Anne paused and glanced back expectantly.

Knapp rushed in, but the thing was not there. Turning, he glimpsed the remains of Nicholas sagging from the wall, just as it fell to the floor, his face smeared with blood and powdery residue from the exploded *gris-gris.*

Knapp turned away from this atrocity with a groan, and noticed that the door adjoining the parlor was open.

Dear God! Anne!" He rushed into the hallway, using the door behind him. The horrid devil was there; it had her by the hand, swinging her arm in a childlike manner.

"Come, Anne Adele! Or is it just 'Anne' to everyone now? Let's go outside and play!"

It tried to pull her away but, hysterical with fear, she hung onto the door jamb for dear life.

"I want you to meet all my friends!"

The creature of evil swung both doors shut, catching her hand between them, and eliciting a mighty shriek of agony.

Knapp dashed to her rescue.

Pulling her inside the parlor, Frater Dementis slammed both doors in Knapp's face. Her dress became caught on a doorknob, tearing some of it from her body.

Knapp tried the doors, but found them jammed tightly shut. He fumed in outraged frustration.

Frater Dementis yanked the rest of the dress from Anne's bodice with one brutal motion. Her wrist broken, she howled in anguish as it led her, terrified beyond any defense, by that hand into the room as if presenting a debutante to society.

It tore a curtain from the window and fastened it around its neck for an elegant cloak. The infernal horror crookedly bowed and gently took both her hands in its own, and, cackling wickedly, started to squeeze slowly.

Anne screamed anew, and didn't stop as the bones of all her fingers crackled and broke, until she fainted.

Frater Dementis then observed his gnarled, limp handiwork, reacting with ghoulish comic surprise and admiration. It kissed her mangled digits and, supporting her at the waist, danced a delicate minuet with the unconscious woman.

"Oh, but of course!" it purred sarcastically. "Miss Anne is no longer a little girl! She's known the pleasure of a man's kiss! A real good-night kiss!"

It's drooling, cretinous lips bussed her tenderly on the mouth, probed with its scabrous tongue...

She awakened, screeching in utter fright.

Knapp entered from the bedroom, poker in hand, but only in time to witness his black-hearted prodigy swinging Anne around and around by the arms with alarming speed.

Knapp knew she would be killed in that instant and felt his blood run cold.

Finally, it let her go with a "Whee-ee-ee!", sending her flying through the window.

"Fornicator!" it screeched after her.

She fell to the ground amidst a shower of glass.

The mad monstrosity giggled with glee.

Knapp's poker felled Frater Dementis with a single, crashing blow across the top of its head. He fingered the poker handle.

In a trice, though bloodied, it twirled itself back upright and clutched Knapp's lapels in its unnatural but vicelike grip.

"A nice try! But you've seen my true face, Knapp! You must certainly die next!"

Knapp brutally whipped the poker against its teetering knees, knocking Frater Dementis to the floor again, and surged out and down the stairs.

He raced through the foyer, down the porch steps and to the hitching rail. He dropped the poker and yanked at the simple loop Nicholas had put in the reins, but only tightened the knot.

"Damn!"

A shadow from inside Maison Duquesne fell over him; he looked to see what it was.

Frater Dementis occupied the doorway.

105

"*Fear me not*, William Knapp!" it cheered grimly.

It lurched out onto the porch and down the steps toward Knapp, stretching its swaying, inverted arms ahead of it, and chortling a reverberating squeal.

Knapp pulled the reins free and bounded up into the carriage driver's seat as the monster scooped up the discarded poker and raised it ominously high while reaching for the bridle. Knapp snapped the reins in its small, insane face and got the skittish team under way in the nick of time, flying from the scene, leaving the abomination on its own doorstep.

A cloud obscured the moon, making all dim below.

The enraged hellion roared incoherently, virtually in tongues, and spewed curses as the Duquesne coach streaked into the deep black of night.

Knapp drove the team hard. The wind stung his face. He fought the emotions churning inside, and dared not look back.

Frater Dementis hobbled to the livery and soothed Nicholas's horse in his master's familiar voice as it walked him to the front. "Easy now, ma *beauté. Ne pas bronchez... C'est moi. C'est moi...* "

The evil genius reversed and pulled up its hood over the limp features of Tristan, basking in the bright, full moonlight as it returned from hiding. Then it tucked the poker under its arm, mounted and rode out.

Moonlit, its cruel little countenance chuckled as its cloak, then hood, were blown back by the whipping winds.

Driving fast as he could, Knapp looked back instinctively.

Frater Dementis was swiftly drawing closer, closer...

As they approached the same crossroads that was the site of the accident caused by Thorndike, Knapp flailed the reins sharply but to little avail. The monster rode up alongside him.

"You're going too fast, Knapp! *You'll have an accident!*"

At the fork, it hurled its poker at Knapp's team. They fell, twisting the carriage over with them, as before. Knapp was thrown from his seat, and rolled over and over on the ground before he came to a painful halt. Still conscious, he battled his arm's increased agony as he tried to raise himself in the pale moonlight.

Frater Dementis appeared, still on horseback, once again blanketing Knapp in its shadow. It tensed as if ready to pounce, but ceased, hearing more people and horses in the vicinity, quickly growing louder.

Two wagons full of citizens on their way to the city and Mardi Gras began to approach the crossroads.

The maddened freak whirled its steed around and, hissing, took to the shadows of the overhanging willows just adjacent to the highway.

"Help! Please! Here!" Knapp called out weakly, unable to place the voice as his own.

"Look! An accident!"; "Stop!"; "Who is it?"; "Help him, Doctor! He's passed out!" and other shouts of alarm went up.

Some revelers poured out of their vehicles, hurrying to the stranger's aid. Among them was Dr. Patterson, dressed as a Roman senator. He and one or two noticed the dark rider streaking off toward the city a short distance away, and all heard the shrill scream: "Damn the Mardi Gras...!"

"What in the name of God was *that?!*" puzzled Patterson.

More voices urged him: "Here he is, Doctor!; "Over here!"; "Don't touch him! He's hurt!"; "Who is he?"

Squatting to take a look, Dr. Patterson announced: "I know this man. He's the stranger I told you about, that doctor Knapp...! Andrew, we'll take him back to your house. It's closest."

Andrew, a lion for the evening, nodded swift agreement. "Yes, of course! Lend a hand!" He summoned other costumed revelers to lift Knapp delicately onto a wagon.

"Careful now," directed Patterson.

The wagons were turned around at the intersection.

***

Chapter Thirteen

Seeing Is Believing

Still keeping vigil on the sill in his loft, and now on his second bottle, Thorndike's fear seemed to have dissipated a little more with every swallow.

"Stupid fools... Don' know anything... Haven't seen what *I've* seen!" he grumbled to himself as he watched the action in the street.

Crequeline Crozaix shuffled by below, in a moving circle of her sect. She stopped and peered up sharply at Thorndike's window. He gave a start. She laughed cheerlessly at him before turning the corner and disappearing down an alley. He gawked down after her, ignoring the street festivities, then nervously backed away from the window.

As the costumed throng circulated noisily to and fro around it, Frater Dementis, no more than a dark-hooded man in a frightening little mask to these revelers, made its way easily through the merry-making at first, occasionally wafting in whichever direction it was pushed. As it followed the crowd in its tentative gait, revelers' feet stepped on its own, and otherwise collided with its mangled limbs. But it was wily enough to keep a straight, immobile face, so that only its searching eyes moved.

"Ooh! Damn you, you fat fool!"

The once-human beast winced with pain, but held its temper to a growl, as Leo Durant, the chubby whitewing, very drunk and masquerading as the Devil, bumped shoulders with the monster, partly dislodging his beard.

"Whoops...! Beg pardon, m'sieur! Say, who are you supposed to be anyway?" he slurred.

"Death!" grinned Frater Dementis.

"No," corrected the street-sweeper, "Death has a skull's face. You're not quite there yet... You look like a pygmy!" he laughed raucously.

Frater Dementis pulled off the Devil's beard, plus a few real whiskers from his mustache, tossed them in his face, and pushed its way into the crowd.

"Ow...!" Leo winced back.

Knapp awoke, sitting up with a start to find himself on a settee in a brightly lit place, surrounded by whispering revelers milling around him in masks and costumes.

He tried to stand up. His arm, now broken and in a new sling, slipped out a bit.

"Arm's broken this time. Sit down."

Knapp saw Senator Dr. Patterson sitting across from him.

"Thank you," said Knapp, groggy with pain.

"Ask him, Doctor!" urged Andrew.

109

"Well, you seem to have a penchant for carriage accidents, Doctor Knapp. I do hope this is just a coincidence."

Knapp, emphatic with remembrance, answered: "No, no! It isn't! There's a mad killer about! He must be found before more innocent people are slaughtered!"

The revelers reacted strongly.

"Who's been slaughtered?" inquired Patterson.

"At Maison Duquesne --!"

The reactions redoubled.

"The recluse Tristan has -- gone insane and slain his sister and his servant, and tried to kill me as well -- in the carriage! I was running for help, for my life! That's why there were two -- two accidents. You must believe me! We've no time -- " He broke off with a sudden realization: "Thorndike! Thorndike the painter will be the next victim!"

"Why, the man's raving!" a harlequin concluded.

Dr. Patterson hushed him.

"No, no! You see, he saw the face...! We all saw the face... He's a killer, a soulless fiend. You must take my word."

"Well, now, we did see somebody," the doctor recalled, " -- or some*thing!*"

"And we heard him too!" a Cleopatra claimed.

Andrew produced the poker. "And we found *this!*"

Knapp got to his feet. "We should call the police immediately! Is there a telephone here?"

"Right this way, Doctor!" Andrew effused. "I'll call them!"

"Tell them to hurry. He's on the loose, God knows where by now."

"I hope the line's clear...! Hello, hello!"

The guests' chatter prevented Knapp from hearing this end of the conversation. He spoke to Patterson. "Doctor, you'd better get to Maison Duquesne and see if either Anne or Nicholas are alive somehow. He's upstairs, and she's -- around the back of the house."

"Very well. But I intend to speak to the police myself first."

"We got through!" Andrew crowed, and handed the telephone and receiver to Knapp, but Dr. Patterson took it.

"Hello, this is Doctor Patterson up at Carrollton. I have a man here claims to be a doctor -- "

"I'm a Professor of Biology at --! Give me that!" Knapp grabbed the earpiece from the doctor, who left in a huff, blaring: "I wash my hands of this crazy man!"

"Hello, this is Professor William Knapp of Boston. I'm calling to report a murderer at large, a madman. I have reason to believe that he's after a man, an artist named Gilbert

Thorndike... in the French Quarter, I believe... No, I don't know the address. You'll have to find him. The man is in grave danger, believe me! And so am I if he finds out I'm alive -- Who?! The madman, the madman!" Then, more patiently: "Professor William Erasmus Knapp, K-n-a-p-p. Boston, yes, Boston University. I teach Biology and wrote a book on the subject of psycho-- *'Describe the madman'...?"* He took a deep breath.

At that same time, Madeleine, Karl, Korbecz and some other Bohemians were drunkenly climbing the wooden stairs to their friend's loft. Karl swilled directly from a bottle, yelling: "He's asleep, I tell you!"

"How could he be sleeping? It's impossible!" Madeleine proclaimed.

"Where else could he be then?" asked the Aryan as they reached his door.

"Well, let's find out!" she smiled, and knocked. "Thorndike! Gilbert, lover, are you in there?" She tried the door. "It's locked!"

"Bolted," determined Karl. "That means he's here! Thorndike!"

"You'll miss Mardi Gras!" gurgled Korbecz.

"Thorndike!" called Madeleine again. "We know you're in there!

"Go away! I'm -- ill!" he hollered back.

A few of them scoffed out loud.

"You sound drunk as usual to me!" Korbecz joked.

"I -- I'll join you tomorrow night!"

"No, you won't! You'll join us right now or never again...! Thorndike!" The others joined her in calling him out. "Come out!" she continued. "We have a mask for you!"

He huddled closer into the corner with his bottle and implored: "Go away! I want no mask, no -- executioner's hood... I want you to leave me alone!"

"Oh, but, Thorndike! You will miss all the fun! My company!" She tried it in French: *Gilbert...? Ouvrez la porte, Gilbert...!* Then: "Oh, for Christ's sake, Thorndike!"

They all chanted his name.

Directly below, Frater Dementis heard the name, grinned just a little, and worked its way closer to the building's open door...

"Thorndike!" they cried, "Come out, for God's sake!" And ultimately: "Ah, to Hell with him!"

It entered the apartment building, closed the front door, and stealthily ascended the stairs.

"Thorndike, this is your last chance!' Karl boomed.

"Oh, enough!" spat Madeleine. "I've had my fill of his moods! We're giving you up for dead, do you hear?!"

The Bohemians started downstairs. Halfway up, Frater Dementis smiled and pushed Korbecz over the bannister. The others stopped short. More or less unhurt, the fat man sat up on the floor and fidgeted a bit, looking for wounds.

"*Hey!* What did you do *that* for?!" Karl demanded.

The monster peered up at them, its face lit by an electric wall-lamp between it and them; Madeleine screamed at the sight.It hurled two more

112

inebriates into each other, rendering them both unconscious; they fell to the floor.

It smashed the lamp with its fist, darkening the stairway and most of the landing above.

"What is it? What's going on out there?" Thorndike wanted to know.

Karl rushed down the steps to confront the monster. It pushed his face against the broken lamp, then took and poured his bottle over his head, electrocuting the blond Bohemian in a literal flash.

It then threw Karl's body down the stairs and turned its attention to Madeleine. The remaining Bohemians scrambled for the door, shouting: "Help, help! Help, murder!"

She screamed as Frater Dementis reached her. The creature snatched a thick handful of her hair and, carrying her back up to the landing, dislodged the railing with a savage kick of one crooked foot. Then it swung the poor girl around in a perfect arc, twice, and then, after suspending her in mid-air a moment, pitched her to the floor below. She fell on Korbecz, who was just rising to his feet. The two ran for the door and escaped while Frater Dementis continued up to the landing, past the others out cold on the floor.

"The Devil! The Devil's in there!" Madeleine screeched.

"Up there! Wearing a mask!" warned Korbecz, now sober.

The street revelers retorted: "We're *all* masked!"; "You're drunk."; "Or crazy!"; "And so are we!"; "Yes, join us!"

"Besides, I'm right here!" added Leo Durant.

"No, listen!" Madeleine pleaded.

In the loft, Thorndike backed away from the door and ducked behind a statue.

A moment later, his door was pounded in with one blow as if by a battering-ram, the beam as well as the door splintered.

Frater Dementis entered, meandering about almost playfully.

"Thorndike...! Gilbert Thorndike...! Such a face should not be hidden from view!" it cajoled.

Thorndike shivered. The gleeful nemesis picked up the sculptor's hammer and chisel from the workbench behind it.

"Will you sit for me, sir...?"

Thorndike screamed and bolted for the broken doorway, but Frater Dementis whirled into his path, catching the artist with both upside-down arms. Face-to-face with the monstrous, shrunken face, he writhed to escape its clutches. Then the thing spun its posture back somehow, making it the former Tristan who now faced and seized the reckless artist.

"I must immortalize that face --!"

Thorndike, aghast and energized, broke free, but, tripping and sliding over discarded bottles, fell back against his easel.

Frater Dementis raised the tools and moved toward him...

At his open front door, Andrew tried to restrain the Boston man from leaving. "But if he's as dangerous as you say, --!"

"You simply don't understand!" Knapp protested. "I've got to be there! To aid the police in their search! I *know* this creature, this man --! *Please* let me borrow your carriage!"

"But they're on their way *here* as well! They'll be only a minute, I'm sure!"

"Yes, all right, then. I'll wait."

"*This* man's mad is what *I* think!" Dr. Patterson opined, sipping some peach brandy.

Two policemen arrived at the shabby apartment building on foot, Madeleine and Korbecz in tow.

"In there!" she pointed. "Be very careful!"

"The man's insane!" Korbecz said unnecessarily.

114

"Show us this loft," ordered one of the officers.

"Oh, no, not me! Not in there!" Korbecz cowered.

"It's not safe! The man *is* mad and very strong!" Madeleine convinced them.

Distracted by each other, none of them saw the black-clad figure that darted from the front entrance into a cluster of passersby.

"Maybe we should wait for reinforcements..." thought one officer.

Knapp rode with two policemen in their paddy-wagon, going quite fast. They hit a bump; Knapp flinched.

"How'd it happen? This madman of yours?" asked one Officer Murtaugh.

"I'll try to have it make sense..." Knapp began, "though I don't understand it all myself."

Another policeman arrived on a bicycle and leaned it against an alley wall. The other policemen and Bohemians converged with him outside Thorndike's building. After a briefing, the first two officers on the scene entered the building cautiously. The bicycle patrolman remained outside, preventing curious partiers from gathering.

Inside, the two policemen viewed the carnage on and around the staircase. Besides Karl's corpse, there were two more out cold. One officer addressed the policeman outside: "Get an ambulance. We're going up." They started to climb...

At the landing above, they eyed with awe the damaged doorway, and, looking inside, a sight they'd never forget.

The officers moaned and retched seeing Gilbert Thorndike's chisel, having been driven into his skull many times over, resting in his temple. His body was festooned with two dozen paintbrushes sticking out at every angle, and streaked with splashes of paint and dripping blood. And the cadaver was stood upright on its very own canvas and easel, a ghastly work of Art.

The current Rex rode by in his magnificent carriage, greeted by the myriad, peculiar false faces who clamored for his "gold" and other gifts, as policemen gathered, conferred and searched about the vicinity.

Frater Dementis moved with difficulty through the teeming masses. Its face lowered, curtain-cloak gathered around its arms, the murderous monstrosity was buffeted painfully back and forth, again and again, then finally, inadvertently crowded into a mirrored storefront.

It regarded its own image with surprise. Blood and paint decorated the cloak, but the monster only saw the horror of its own self. Enraged anew, Frater Dementis turned from the mirror, facing the flow of people with a deep breath of perverse contentment.

Then, a cutting whisper from behind: "You're going to kill them all, are you?"

Frater Dementis wheeled around; no one was there. Then, it felt the hood expand with breath. Then, the hood was blown off by a fierce gust of Tristan's breath.

"Yes, it's Tristan!"

The entity saw its own fear in the mirror and turned away again, backing up against the locked door behind it.

"You were right, my brother... We did both go mad, but become as one -- *we did not!*"

Tristan fought his alter ego's attempt to replace the hood.

"No, you won't lose me so easily, brother!" He laughed cruelly as Frater Dementis whimpered in panic, desperately trying to cover its other face. One of the twisted hands was bitten; the creature's blood-caked fingers cringed and withdrew.

"We'll never stop growing mad, you see! We'll always be right here, together! Growing madder and madder together – *Together!*"

Tristan laughed merrily. "Oh, remember the fun we had? I do! – How you laughed! And how I wept! Remember, brother? Remember all our precious horror and endless terror? I remember everything! And so do you...! And now we *know* everything! We'll make quite a mark on society, you and I!"

The Voice returned, trying to reason with his other self: "No... Stop punishing us... You're behaving as Father would have done."

"You mean *my* father!" argued Tristan. "*Your* father is *Knapp!*"

"We have suffered enough!"

"I disagree! I need to hear your death-rattle in my throat!" Tristan seethed.

Reflected in the mirror, the Face registered prescient pity.

"You will," it lamented. "You've gone too far yourself... They'll kill us like a mad dog in the street."

"*I never asked for this! I didn't want things this way!*"Tristan ranted, before an almost amusing notion occurred: "Could it be that *no one* wanted things this way...?"

By then, several passersby had stopped to witness this strange scene. The Face tried to cover itself.

Tristan laughed insanely. "Go ahead and show them, brother! We have no secrets now, have we? Go and claim our rightful place in society!"

Livid with torment, Frater Dementis raised the hood and pushed itself into the crowd while Tristan laughed on with weary disgust.

"Look at that!"; "What a wonderful costume!"; "Yes, and that frightening mask!" the onlookers commented.

On another Tenderloin street, Knapp arrived in the police wagon.

"Let's go, Professor," said Officer Murtaugh. Both officers and he got out and looked around at all the uninhibited hoopla. A sergeant wandered over to them.

"You say he attacks anyone who sees his face?" Murtaugh asked.

"Hold up a second, Officer," the sergeant interrupted, pointing to Knapp. "I'm Sergeant Roth. You talking about this madman we've been looking for?"

"Yes, Sergeant," answered Knapp. "I'm the one who notified you. Didn't you get a description of your quarry from your superior?"

"Who's this, Murtaugh?"

"This is Professor Knapp. We brought him down from Carrollton. Trouble at Maison Duquesne."

"I see... Well, Professor, yes, we did get the description you gave to Headquarters," the sergeant confided, "but it is just a wee bit hard to believe!"

An upside-down hand tapped him on the shoulder; he turned. Crooked fingers clenched and unclenched beside the unearthly hooded face.

"Seeing is believing!" Distorted thumbs reached for the sergeant's eyes.

Knapp experienced yet more shock, hearing the scream.

The luckless policeman fell to his knees in anguish, holding his face, blood seeping through his fingers.

The other officers were stunned. More revelers began to circle around, soon forming a buzzing crowd.

Frater Dementis wiped its thumbs on its cloak with exaggerated fussiness. Then it recognized Knapp and gasped.

"Ah...! Come to the Mardi Gras, have you, Knapp? Good! I0 get to kill you again!" It advanced slowly, menacingly.

Tristan laughed again from within the hood. Momentarily confused, Frater Dementis's steps faltered.

Rallying themselves, the shaken police officers brandished their weapons. "Stop right there, you!"; "And take off that mask!"

Frater Dementis turned to face the policemen.

From the crowd, one voice broke the stillness; it was Madeleine's: *"It's not a mask!"*

Dozens shuddered as one.

Exalted, the mad menace assailed the heavens with upraised fists in a chilling roar of both rage and fulfillment.

The crowd began to panic.

"Stop that this instant!" shrieked Frater Dementis.

They all fell silent.

Frater Dementis smiled sweetly, turning to acknowledge Knapp, who felt both despair and revulsion, tears streaming down his cheeks. The living nightmare stepped boldly up to him, smoothly shoving a policeman aside. Then it held its index finger, askew but aloft, up to his terror-stricken face.

"You cry too much!" it spoke in Knapp's own voice.

Then it clutched him by the collar, chuckling nastily, snarling with irony: "Why, Knapp, look at me! It's the first time I've laughed in years!" It started twisting the collar.

A shot rang out, catching the fiend by surprise. Its hood fell back with the recoil. The mad Tristan, alert again, laughed unpleasantly. The crowd gasped.

The policeman who fired from the ground took careful aim again. "Stop!"

Frater Dementis swayed, growling at his former friend and mentor.

Another shot hit home. It whirled about and crumpled, still hanging onto Knapp's collar. Tristan's face was now before his. Frater Dementis choked and sputtered. Both were dying.

"Dear Lord!" exclaimed Knapp. "Tristan, I'm sorry... I couldn't know -- everything."

Tristan smiled regretfully at him.

"Damn the Mardi Gras!" Frater Dementis cursed from behind.

"It is the worst time of year," Tristan groaned, ultimately their last words.

119

"Hold your fire!" Murtaugh shouted. "I got him!" He leapt into action, clubbing the wounded creature to the ground with one well-measured blow.

It crashed at Knapp's feet, the broken bones spreading the body formlessly for a moment, unseen beneath the curtain-cloak, before regrouping in unknowable anguish. It rolled over, making both faces visible to all within range.

Infuriated, Frater Dementis moaned, squirming and thrashing in the dirty street, futilely clutching at Murtaugh's shoe.

More policemen circled around.

Knapp's face now hung, nearly lifeless, weary with horror.

"What the Hell is this thing?!" somebody blurted. Another threw a stone at the misshapen thing on the ground. Next, the crowd moved in like a locust swarm. The wretched carcass was pelted by the outraged mob with everything available: sticks, stones, bottles, masks... Someone struck at it with a buggy whip.

"Look at it!"; "It's Satan himself!"; "Hellspawn!"; "Filthy monster!"; "Kill it!"; "Kill the monster!" they yowled.

The fracas continued vigorously until a policeman fired twice into the air. The crowd fell quieter by degrees and retreated from the site of the smashed and bleeding form, still moving, still dying. Then the officer lowered his firearm deliberately, aiming for the head.

Knapp, though feeling utterly helpless, cried: "Oh, no...!"

The curious crowd buzzed anew.

The policeman waited. "Stay back!"

But they only drew closer.

"No, please don't, officer, please –!" begged Knapp. "Let him die with *some* dignity...! This was once a brave boy."

"I said 'Stay back', you people!" He aimed skyward and pulled the trigger, but found his gun empty.

120

Someone had a pitchfork. The body was poked, jabbed, kicked and overturned into the gutter. A frivolous mood began to ripple through the masked Mardi Gras mob.

"No, it's not a mask, is it?"; "How hideous!"; "What is it"'; "Who is it?"; "Is it human?"; "Get a torch!"

Someone emptied a full bottle of wine over the writhing Frater Dementis, then another dousing followed.

More police arrived, but were hard-pressed to control this situation.

Knapp had to lean back against the paddy wagon to keep from fainting.

"Here's a torch!"; "Give it here!"

The twitching thing was set afire. The immediate crowd backed up, leaving enough room between them and it.

"It's still alive!"; "Burn the ugly thing!"; "Kill the freak!"; "Kill the monster!" they demanded, frenzied.

Consumed by flames, the various voices of Frater Dementis screamed in agony, arching itself into a fiery bridge. A cheer went up from the crowd.

"Yes, let it burn!"; "Kill it!"; "Is it dead?"; "Make sure it's dead!"; "What a sight!"

"I'm not cleaning *that* up!" muttered Leo Durant.

Part of the crowd gave way for medics from Charity Hospital's ambulance. They carried a stretcher to the body, still afire. One kicked dirt on it to extinguish the flames. Another escorted the blinded Sergeant Roth to their conveyance.

Knapp watched the triumph of the mob indifferently now, completely drained and benumbed. Murtaugh rejoined him.

"You all right, Professor?"

Knapp nodded almost imperceptibly.

"I want you to come with me to Headquarters, sir. We have -- many questions."

"Very well," Knapp agreed.

A burly medic came up to them and pointed to the dazed Knapp. "You come along with us." He adjusted his sling. "Get this arm tended to... You ready, sir?"

Knapp didn't answer, prompting the medic to ask the officer: "Is he still with us?"

"Still with you, young man," he returned. "I'm just a little tired... of questions."

"He's coming with me," Murtaugh told the medic.

They hoisted him up into the paddy wagon. He looked through the small aperture in time to see medics drop the still-smouldering body onto the stretcher. Then he looked away and closed his eyes...

***

Chapter Fourteen

Sometimes Tragedies Help

Professor W. E. Knapp sat motionless at his desk in the Homerian Society, oblivious to his everyday colleagues also present. Some warmed themselves at the wide, welcoming hearth, as outdoors, Winter lingered.

He needed sleep, he realized, but Celia was waiting. She wanted to tell him all about her wedding plans, and he would help her make decisions. He couldn't fail to meet her. She'd been so kind, so understanding and supportive this past year, since he'd returned from what he'd repeatedly called his 'vacation in Hades'.

He felt as though he'd spent the entire twelve months talking, explaining, trying to explain, to seemingly everybody, what had happened to the now-infamous Tristan Duquesne of New Orleans, Louisiana, and his own involvement in that affair, that failed experiment.

Knapp still battled bouts of guilty depression. So many lives had been ruined, all so meaninglessly, all ending in such arbitrary misfortune and flagrant violence.

He stared down at his open journal, still lost in thought. Then he read what he'd just written back to himself:

"It's Mardi Gras time once again in New Orleans. And I shall be visiting there again this year, and every year at this time, and every day of the year, but especially now, against my will -- for I shall never really leave that time nor place. Memories of that tragedy, that evil last day will ever linger within me.

Yet how clearly I remember those most comforting words: "Do not fear these mysteries, William. You must continue your studies of the inner mind, --
"

He looked away, at the fireplace, and watched as through smoky sworls emerged the faces of Nicholas, Anne and a smiling, hopeful Tristan Duquesne.

" -- although its secrets may be both wondrous and tragic. Sometimes tragedies help... " he recited quietly, closing his eyes. The faces vanished...

The wrathful countenance of Frater Dementis loomed suddenly: *"Fear me not, William Knapp!"*

Its bone-jarring laugh jolted Knapp fully awake.

And there was Celia --!

Knapp sighed with great relief. She took his hand.

Jonas, standing by, asked: "Are you feeling all right, Professor?"

He squeezed her hand, and said, humbly but confidently: "The work goes on, Jonas. The work goes on..."

He rose, donned hat and coat, took his journal and Celia's arm, and together they left.

***

124

ABOUT THE AUTHOR

Joe Alaskey

Emmy Award Winner and Best Selling Author, Joe Alaskey, whose Internet Movie Database page and resume reads like a *Who's Who* of Hollywood, has enjoyed an illustrious career as one of the most sought after voice-over artists in the TV and Film industry, as well as memorable performances as an actor for Film, TV, Radio and Stage.

A theatrical veteran and comedy circuit regular, Joe Alaskey was plucked from the stage and comedy clubs in the 80s to star in the motion picture *Lucky Stiff*, directed by Anthony Perkins, and won a place in the hearts of millions as the lovable Uncle Beano on the science fiction situation comedy, *Out of This World*. A fixture on 80s television, he was the co-star of *Couch Potatoes* and guest starred on countless shows including *Head of the Class, Night Court, Nurses, Hollywood Squares* and *The Match Game*.

Joe Alaskey took the animation world by storm voicing hundreds of animation projects for Television and Film, including *The Looney Tunes, Steven Spielberg Presents Tiny Toon Adventures, Tom & Jerry, Duck Dodgers, Sponge Bob Squarepants, Sylvester and Tweety Mysteries, The Rugrats, All Grown Up, Looney Tunes Back In Action, The Garfield Show, Forest Gump and Casper*, to name a few. Joe Alaskey has written stage plays, TV and radio scripts, as well as *The Wild, Wild West Show* for Six Flags Over Texas and *1958: A Retrospeculation*, an ambitious and energetic one-man stage play he starred in at the Steve Allen Theatre.

Joe Alaskey is the best-selling author of *That's Still Not All, Folks!!* (Bear Manor Media) and Queasy Street: Volume One - Eleven Tales of Fantasy (Hash Tag Publishing) He is currently the voice of the narrator on the television series *Murder Comes To Town* for the Investigation Discovery Network. Visit him online www.JoeAlaskey.com

Joe Alaskey
Social Media

www.JoeAlaskey.com
Facebook.com/JoeAlaskeyFans
Facebook.com/QueasyStreet
Facebook.com/FraterDementis

Show Your Frater Dementis Pride With A Book Bag Hoodie or Shirt

Give The Neighborhood A Scare!!
Wear Me If You Dare!!

Frater Dementis Online Store
CafePress.com/FraterDementis